Mothic Wreckage

Anya Nagle

Published by Anya Nagle, 2024.

MOTHIC WRECKAGE

First edition. January 27, 2024.

Copyright © 2024 Anya Nagle.

ISBN: 979-8223476382

Written by Anya Nagle.

ONE

N ot to jinx it or anything, but I'd say it's going well so far.
I lean forward and kiss her again, harder this time, allowing her hands to trace up and down my back. I'm sweaty, of course. I just got done hopping around onstage for an hour and a half. If she cares, she doesn't show it. She is pretty, this girl. Her fingernails claw at my skin, asking to be let in. It is hot where we are, the two of us stuffed into the corner of the backstage bathroom.

She's not the first. I doubt she'll be the last. I've hooked up with fans before — there was a pretty redhead in Tulsa, who wore a strawberry necklace and smelled like Chanel No. 5. There was the blue-eyed girl from Palo Alto, with box-dyed purple hair cut into a sharp, exclamatory bob. And who could forget the prettiest of them all, Lily, my best friend — who'd come to see the show once, about a year and a half ago. She and I had seen each other afterward, smiled, and I'd let her lead me behind the building and have all the fun she wanted. It was a nice reunion. We parted as friends, of course, and we still FaceTime every night. There wasn't anything substantial about it — we were both bored — but I was happy she was there.

Then there was Piper. I don't like to think about Piper.

"Oh, Stars," this girl murmurs, sounding emotional. She looks at me with doe-like brown eyes. The tiny tattoos on her skin drive me insane. "I think I'm dreaming."

I kiss her again. "No, not a dream," I say. "It's too good for a dream." I wish I had remembered to ask for her name before we started. It would be weird to ask for it now.

After she and I finish up, we sit next to each other on the dirty bathroom tiles. I wipe my glasses off on the hem of my shirt. Ocelle got this shirt for me on the night of our first big show. It's a black button-down with short sleeves, nothing fancy, but on the inside pocket, where only I could ever see it, Ocelle had hand-embroidered *SING GOOD*.

Unfortunately, my throat didn't always want to take that advice, but it always gave me a good laugh and helped me loosen up before a show.

I stare at it now. *Sing good.* Next to me, the girl pulls out her phone and taps through a couple of messages from someone named *bae <3*.

"What are you doing later?" she asks me, not looking up.

"I don't know." I lean my head back against the wall. I catch a glimpse of myself in the mirror; my face is a little puffy, somehow still pretty. "I think the others wanted to grab some dinner, so... we might find a local spot and smoke a little after. We'll see how we feel."

"Nice." She does look at me now, her cheeks flushing as she smiles. "You know, you guys did great tonight."

"Thanks."

She stands and pulls her shirt back on. It is waiting for her, tossed haphazardly over the sink. "I should probably get going. My friends are wondering where I went."

"What a story you'll have for them," I say.

"They'll never believe me." Her slender arms, encircled with charm bracelets, glint in the yellowish light. "Thanks again for a cool night, Stars."

"Hey, wait," I say, standing as she makes her way to the door. I finish pulling my jeans back on. "Uh...what was your name again?"

She blinks at me, startled, and laughs. "You mean you forgot?" she teases.

"Maybe."

"That's okay." She brushes a lock of wavy blonde hair behind her ear, revealing an earring shaped like a smiley face. "Greta."

"Greta," I repeat. The word is like honey on my tongue. "Well, Greta, it was very nice to meet you."

"You too." Then Greta is gone, and I'm alone in the bathroom of the Borealis in Provo, Utah. I shift my weight. Annabel has always scoffed at my after-show tendencies, calling me a long-lost remnant of the rock-and-roll era, but honestly I just get sad after shows. I need someone to hold like they belong to me, and who am I going to hold? Annabel? Ocelle? No chance.

It's okay to be lonely. And it is in the embrace of these girls that I am the loneliest, the edges of my glasses digging into the skin of their shoulders.

That's how it was with Piper. I started dating her, the lead singer of another band called Aphrodite's Kisses, about a year after Mothic Wreckage released its debut album. For a long time, things were good, almost normal — I felt okay in someone's arms again. It was easy to nestle my face into the crook of her neck and just breathe for a change. I was happy.

I wash my face with water of questionable quality and leave the bathroom, smelling of Greta and her sweat. In the green room, Ocelle and Kento, our newbie drummer, are playing cards. (They knew each other before the band, and Ocelle is the one who introduced Kento to us this past year. "You're just gonna love this guy, he's a beast on the drums. Not so good at DDR, though. I kicked his *ass*.") Annabel is FaceTiming Chris, her boyfriend back home. That leaves me, sitting in the middle of the room, picking at my hands and wondering what's left to do.

It's not like they don't notice me when I come back in, and it's not like they don't know what I was doing. There's no use playing pretend.

"Well, well," Ocelle says. "If it isn't Romeo. How was it, champ?"

"Fine." I take a seat.

Annabel looks up from her phone to glare at me. "You shouldn't make a habit of that, Stars," she warns. "It's a dangerous idea."

I fall silent.

"Oh, let him have his fun." Ocelle gets up from his card game and twirls toward me, leaving Kento looking aggravated in the corner. "What was her name? You did remember to *ask* this time, didn't you?"

"Yeah." Her lingering touch still burns on my skin, the faint odor of lavender. "Her name was Greta."

Ocelle sits next to me, leaning in close. He smells the same as he always does, a combination of weed and cologne, and then a whiff of something like the seaside.

"Well, glad you enjoyed it," he says, clapping me on the shoulder. "What would you say to some dinner?"

"You guys can go on ahead." I grab my guitar and balance it on my knee. "I'll probably just stick around here and write a little before I head back to the hotel."

Kento knits his eyebrows. "Are you sure?" he asks. I nod.

After a couple of more minutes, Ocelle grows bored of trying to convince me, so he leads Annabel and Kento out to the street. I look at my guitar, trying to remember what it had been like the first time I'd ever touched it. It was in a display case at the Brace Pond Music Shop back home, gorgeous and shiny and angelic, and the strings seemed to glow whenever I strummed. Lately, though, I've felt reluctant. It used to be that while I was playing my guitar, a small part of me would come back and everything would feel okay again, but now it feels sinful, sacrilegious maybe, to even hold it. Cal used to be here, listening to me while I played my guitar. He used to ask me if he could paint on it, and I'd always say no. What I wouldn't give for him to paint on it now, a little piece of him that would stick with me forever.

I've been writing a song about him. The way he asked me to. I don't have much — a couple chords and maybe a verse or two — but I think he'd like what I have. It's a lot harder than it looks. I wring my hands out.

I play a dissonant chord, waiting for the sound to mean something.

TWO

That was what he'd wanted me to call it. Mothic Wreckage. He didn't know if there was truly such a word as *mothic* — of or relating to moths — and he was too lazy to ever go and look it up.

"Who cares if someone has already decided it's a word?" he said to me one afternoon, leaning back against the cracked wall of our apartment and sticking a Lucky Strike between his teeth. He was so fiercely independent, so annoyingly suave. "It's your word now."

For a long time I'd told him no, no — *Mothic Wreckage* is no name for a band. I needed something classic and nostalgic, something that would make a modern audience yearn for a romanticized past. *Mothic Wreckage* only invoked the disturbing imagery of fires set to empty living rooms, cities falling apart, and a world encased in bugs. There was no beauty there, at least none that I saw, but then again, that was the difference that so greatly separated me from Cal. I saw beauty where it hid, spreading itself through cracks, fecund and able to be saved, and he saw beauty where there was none.

Mothic Wreckage was my last gift to him. I gave the words back. I sat holding his hand in the dim, listening to the quiet, trying to ignore the thrumming aches of my heart. "Mothic Wreckage," he'd pleaded to me, his eyes bloodshot in the dark. "You love me, right? You'd do that for me, wouldn't you?"

I don't know why it mattered so much, even now. But I nodded. I was never keen on empty promises. It was never even part of the question whether or not I would keep my word.

That was three years ago — maybe four. No, four in August. Just before I'd met Ocelle.

The day after Cal's funeral, which consisted of nothing but sniffling and wilting bouquets (and none of my family showed up — not a one), I decided to go to the record store. I wanted something old. James Brown, maybe, or Aretha Franklin. I would decide when I got there.

Conan's was the name. It was a little old squat brick building squished in between two others, the local thrift store and a Mexican place called Orejas Rojas. No one would ever hang out on this block on purpose unless they were homeless or at my level of bored and depressed, so it was no wonder it felt like a ghost town. Receipts and scattered plastic bags kissed the wind as they rolled. Puddles shone in the damp. A couple of stray cats fought over the remnants of a burger on the sidewalk. It was just before dusk, and the sky had yawned and stretched out its arms to become a sulky purple-orange.

I drew my leather jacket tight around my shoulders and glanced up. I wondered if Cal had made this sky, another one of his paintings, just for me. If so, he'd done a terrific job. My stomach churned at the thought of his paintbrush against the clouds, the scritch-scritch of the horsehair, and the soft, velveteen plush it met.

Conan's was a tiny place, equally as disgusting inside as on the outside. In the fifties and sixties, it had been the most popular place in town, filled to the brim with dancing bobby-soxers and even a milk-shake bar. Nowadays it was the type of place the high-schoolers spread rumors about — chant Buddy Holly's name three times and he'll appear in the bathroom mirror, blah blah blah. A teenage girl with hoop earrings chewed a massive wad of gum and hummed to Freddie Mercury as she wiped the sticky front counter. Her cheeks were all puffed out like a chipmunk's. She barely even glanced at me when I walked in. She struck me as the type of girl who'd dress like the men she was attracted to. Sure enough, she was standing there in a big chunky shirt and men's jeans.

I don't even know what I was really looking for. The aisles were dusty and cramped, and the selection was horrifically unsorted. I saw Jimmy Eat World next to Weezer, Bruno Mars nestled beside Gene Kelly in *An American in Paris*. Perhaps it was all a business ploy, all scrambled like a scavenger hunt to make customers stay longer. If so, I fell for it, self-consciously stepping over wads of hair, unknown discolored patches, lint and lollipop sticks on the green-and-white tile floor. My sneakers squeaked. Their echoing taunts made me cringe, the sound rubbing uncomfortably against my ears. I'd pick up a record, turn it to the B-side, examine it, tasting each track name in my mouth like sugar, but the sweetness always died. Every album, every vinyl, every boxed collector's set was a total facade, disguising what truly lay beneath, which wasn't any more impressive. There was something so unreal about everything. Underneath it all, I suppose, music is nothing but someone saying *help me, help me, help me.*

The record players they had on sale were cheap. I almost took home a beautiful sage-green one from Crosley, mint and shiny in its case, before the teenage clerk hollered at me from across the store that it was on hold. Feeling frustrated, I'd turned around to argue and say that wasn't made apparent at all, but she'd already returned to her Archie comic.

Outside the sun was beginning to set. The yellow fluorescent lights overhead flickered. My eyes ached in their sockets; my hands tingled with the cold coming from the vents. I didn't want to leave without buying anything, but I also didn't feel like sticking around, so I threw myself into the next aisle — which happened to be a random plethora of Jimi Hendrix, U2, and Lana Del Rey. I stared at a couple of them for a long time. My heart felt heavy in my chest, and I couldn't distinguish why. Maybe it was because Cal should have been there, his arms around my waist, his chin on my shoulder.

"Let's go home," he'd complain. "It's late, and I'm hungry, and I have to wash my hair."

"One more minute," I'd say. "Just trying to pick."

He was not there. He was busy with his brushes in the sky, of course. The artist.

I stopped in front of an old favorite: James Gates. *The Wild One.* His pearly white smile grinned at me from the cover. I had about three copies of this record at home, but I could never take my eyes off of it when I saw it out and about. I ran my hands over it and remembered us dancing to it: our socked feet against the hardwood of our kitchen floor, slipping and spinning as we laughed and laughed, not caring about the neighbors and their noise complaints.

"Gates, huh," said an airy voice next to me. I turned and saw him. He had seemingly appeared from thin air, but he was looking at *The Wild One* sagely, as if he'd been standing there for thousands of years. "I never could get into him much."

He looked at me. His eyes were dark with eyeshadow, and his wild curly hair came past his shoulders in an outrageous, crazy flurry. A mustache sat upon his upper lip, and his clavicle was barely visible through all of his jewelry. When he saw me studying him so intently, his eyebrows furrowed.

"I said, *I never could get into him much*," he said, like I was deaf. "Parlez-vous français?"

I blinked. "Sorry." I turned back to the record and grabbed it off the shelf, creating a cloud of dust. "He's always been my favorite."

Turn, one, two, three, dip...and I'd spin him around.

"How come?" the stranger asked.

"I don't know." I was turning the record over and over in my hands without realizing it. "I just like his artistry. He made the kind of music I'd like to make one day."

This made the man change his stance, leaning back on one foot and crossing his arms. "A musician, huh," he said with a seemingly distasteful air, studying me up and down. "You don't look like one. What do you play?"

"Guitar, mostly."

"Oh, bull*shit*. You are not a guitar player."

"What? Yes, I am," I said, fighting the urge to be offended.

The stranger laughed and shook his head, revealing a smile even more stunning than James Gates's. "No, you look more like a piano guy to me," he said. "Hey, man, there's no shame in it. I admire anyone with flexible enough hands to tackle a piano. Me, I'm content to just punch some basslines and call it a night." He held out a hand covered in tiny tattoos, nail-polished fingers glinting in the light. "My name's Ocelle."

I shifted the record to my left arm and shook his hand. "I'm Stars," I said.

"Stars?" Ocelle repeated, snorting. "What kind of name is Stars?"

"Well, what kind of name is Ocelle?"

He let out a loose, haughty laugh. "Well, I'll have you know," he said, "that Ocelle is a term of endearment in Latin. A *my darling* sort of situation, if you will. The apple of your eye."

I internally groaned. Great, another uppity Classics student from the college. The conversation was already getting tired.

"Well, congratulations," I said tonelessly. "My name's Stars and I am way less interesting than you are. You win."

Ocelle grinned like this pleased him. "You buying that Gates shit?" he asked, nodding at the record in my arms. "Man, don't bother. C'mon, it's on me."

"Huh?"

Without a warning of any sort, he grabbed my wrist and started dragging me, stumbling, over to the clerk. She looked at us with bored, half-lidded eyes. Her nametag read *Hi! My Name Is JEANINE.*

Ocelle plucked the record from my grasp as easily as if he was harvesting apples from a tree. He slid it over the counter to Jeanine with a polite but dramatic smile.

"You don't have to pay for it," I murmured to him. "I mean, I don't even know you."

"Not yet," Ocelle teased.

Jeanine rang us up, looking a little less than enthused, and then we were back outside. Just Ocelle, strange Ocelle, and I, beneath Cal's sky, watching the old man who owned Orejas Rojas chasing out a couple of loiterers.

Ocelle turned to look at me again. The wind blew, making a tornado of his long hair, rustling the plastic bag in my hands. "I like you, *Stars*," he said with a smile. "I think we ought to be friends."

"Is that so?" I challenged. "You're a stranger. And you haven't exactly been nice to me since we started talking."

"I'm dramatic. That was then, this is now. Besides, I just bought you that lovely record, didn't I?" As if to prove his point, he flipped some hair over his shoulder. "Don't take it too personally."

"Alright."

"So, Mr. Music Man." Ocelle picked at some chipped nail polish on his middle finger. "You play anywhere in town? I'd like to stop by one of your sets sometime."

"Yeah. A couple of times a month. I've got one coming up at the end of next week at Taylor's."

"Cool, I'll be there," he said easily, still not looking at me. "What name do you play under? Let me guess: Spock? Galactus?"

Annoyance bubbled in my stomach. "No."

Old cars drove by, the sunset glinting bronze off their red and white paint. The lights of Conan's marquee dimmed and died. The block was falling asleep, the sky was opening wide, and I was holding a James Gates record and standing across from the most frustratingly fascinating person I'd ever met.

"Okay, so then, what's your stage name?" Ocelle said. "I've got places to be, y'know. Don't make me play Twenty Questions all night long."

"You'll know me when you see me." When I said it, it sounded so right. So correct. Cal was looking at me from somewhere, head tilted, and I felt the wind run across my back like his pleasant hand: "Mothic Wreckage."

THREE

The truth was, I did not have a set next week at Taylor's, so I had to go and ask for one. This adventure had its pros and cons, mostly spearheaded by the double-edged sword of the bunch: one of my only friends, Rigby, owned the joint. Naturally, that meant that as I stepped through the lacquered doors, he was behind the bar picking his teeth with a lollipop stick. He looked at me when I came in, and his face bloomed into a classic Rigby smile, crinkled and worn at the edges but still authentic.

"Look who's come crawling back," he said. "Where'd you come from?"

"My car."

"Funny." He straightened up, fixing his shirtsleeves, and came out from behind the unpopulated bar. In front of me, he was a lot taller, more than I would have liked to admit. His clothes were rumpled and his hair stood up like it had been through a cyclone, but I was glad to see him. He'd been my friend for years, and we'd spent our formative years kissing every girl that complimented us and then brutally rejecting them. "What can I do for you, Stars?"

"I need a set."

"A set, huh..." he said, digging in his pocket and producing a cigarette. "Hey, do you have a lighter on you? Sure, I could give you a set. When?"

"Next Saturday night?"

Rigby winced visibly. "I'm afraid Saturday's a busy night, dude," he said. "I've got a new girl playing Saturday. I could give you Friday unless you're cool with opening for her."

"Sure, whatever. I'll open it. What do I owe you in return?"

He shrugged me off. "Don't worry about it." I watched as he returned to his oasis behind the bar and dug out a notepad, scribbling at the bottom of it: *STARS - OPENING ANNABEL PARK*. "Little pity present from me to you."

"Well, thanks, I guess," I said, craning my neck to see the notepad page better. "Oh, but I won't be performing under my name. I've got a new name."

"Oh, do you?" Rigby yawned and uncapped his pen again. "Hit me with it." I told him, and his eyebrows shot up. "What kinda name is that?"

"Cal chose it."

His sarcastic smirk faded. "Oh," he muttered, busying himself with crossing out *Stars*. "Then I'll see you on Saturday night, Mr. Mothic Wreckage."

I told him thanks and left. Outside, it was starting to rain, and pedestrians were rushing to hide under eaves and umbrellas like suddenly-sprouting flowers. I waited under Taylor's awning and glanced at my forearm, where Ocelle had written his phone number in big blocky letters. He'd casually taken out an Expo marker last night in front of Conan's like he always just carried odd things around like that. And he couldn't have been discreet about it, no; he had to write from wrist to elbow and add smiley faces for garnish. This, I would soon learn, was just the way Ocelle was.

It was an inquisitive little name. *Ocelle*. The large, gaping maw of the *O*, the dancing twinkling light of the French *celle*, a million questions left unasked and unanswered. It was a name befitting its owner, mysterious, flitting in and out of shadows like some sort of dark god.

I walked home and found my apartment in disarray.

That was no one's fault but my own. It was cleaner a few months ago. As I closed the curtains and picked up the throw pillows to put back on the couch, I thought about the set next Saturday night. Opening for someone named Annabel, who I'd forgotten to ask Rigby about at all. I washed dishes and closed my eyes, picturing a high blonde ponytail and intense blue eyes with mile-long lashes. I wasn't sure where the imagery came from. I scrubbed half-heartedly in the sink and thought, again, of Ocelle, of seeing his intense face in the crowd, critical. It would not be me alone there. Just me and my guitar and Ocelle, strange Ocelle. And though I didn't realize it yet, it'd be the beginning of a new era.

That night in my dream I asked Cal, who was sitting across from me as usual, if he thought the set was a good idea.

"Well, sure," he said, his Lucky Strike wobbling as his lips moved. I find it odd that that's the detail that chose to remain, even though it's not what killed him. "It's about time you put yourself out there. I wish you'd done it when I was still here."

"I wish so, too. I think you'd be proud of me."

"I think I'd be proud of you, too." He looked at me sideways. "Are you going to write a song about me?"

"I hadn't thought about it," I admitted. "I can, though. It's never been hard to write about you."

He smiled like this pleased him. "I'll be watching," he reminded me.

"I know."

Waking up had become very difficult. It was hard to watch him disappear again, powerless to do much about it.

—

The place was a lot more packed than I thought it would be. Rigby had promised a fair crowd, but I'm sure we were exceeding the fire safety limit by quite a bit. Backstage, I said hi to Annabel, who was the antithesis of my kitchen table prediction: a tiny Korean girl holding a ukulele decorated with star stickers. She was nice enough, and just before I went onstage shot me a small nod and an almost inaudible, "Good luck".

The stage was small, a little octagon jutting out in the corner of the bar. Some crowded around, others sat at their tables and paid minimal attention. I took a seat on the stool, my guitar resting against my knee.

I felt like melting. I'd never played a set like this before, regardless of what I had or hadn't told Ocelle in front of the record store a week ago. I saw him standing at the bar, holding some ridiculous-looking drink, and he smiled that unreasonably timeless smile at me. If anything, it just made me even more nervous.

I began to strum, and I sang a song I wrote maybe a year ago called "Castle of Girls." It's the sort of sad little guitar ballad you'd expect from someone my age (and with my haircut). It's never been a massive hit, but I played it as if the only person in the room were Cal, and when I opened my eyes again, people were on their feet.

The applause came to me in a dim flushing roar. My voice quivered in my throat, wondering what to say. *Thank you? Here, have another? What else do you want to hear?*

In a flustered daze, I finished the rest of my set (by now I can't even remember what other songs I'd played, just the ending chords of "Castle of Girls" and a pair of eardrums set afire) and wandered to the back room, where Annabel was waiting. She blinked at me from her spot next to the minifridge, arms folded.

"Good job out there," she said. She wasn't necessarily smiling. "Now I'm gonna have to work twice as hard. You know, usually, openers aren't supposed to be that good, right?"

"Well, that's not fair," I murmured, startled. "Plenty of openers are great. Are you trying to take the easy way out?"

She shot me another unreadable look, grabbed her uke from its waiting spot on the loveseat, and headed out.

I curled up in one of Rigby's little easy chairs and checked my phone for any new messages. One from my mom, asking me when I was going to call her — fat chance, the last time I'd texted her had been since before Cal died. One from Ocelle, asking if he could come backstage and say congrats. And one from Lily, my best friend, asking if she'd be welcome to come over for dinner the following night.

Sighing, I swiped up. I opened my mom's message but didn't answer it. I shot back a *yes* to Ocelle and a *yes-but-I'd-have-to-go-grocery-shopping* to Lily.

In no time at all, Ocelle had paraded in and made himself at home. "Oh, Stars, you beautiful intergalactic bastard," he said, draping himself over the dusty loveseat. He was wearing a feather boa over a mesh shirt. "I had no idea such a voice lived in you."

"Thanks, man."

"Don't mention it." He looked at me upside down over the arm of the couch, pushing curly bangs off of his forehead. "But that still didn't make you any more of a guitar player."

I fought the urge to be offended. Again. I would later discover this would be a theme with Ocelle. "What are you talking about?"

"Don't get me wrong, you're a monster on the guitar," Ocelle said airily, "but I just *know* you're a piano guy at heart."

"Okay."

"Is that an 'okay' as in 'you're right' or an 'okay' as in 'please shut the fuck up, Ocelle'?"

"The second one." I tossed him my pick, and he caught it without hardly even looking up.

We sat there in silence for a few minutes, Ocelle having seemingly obeyed. When the crowd cheered and Annabel re-emerged, I told her congrats, even though I'd heard not a single chord of her music.

She gestured with a nod to Ocelle. "Who's this?"

Ocelle stood, clearly delighted at the presence of a new friend. Like a gentleman from the wrong era, he took Annabel's hand in his and kissed it, introducing himself. "And you are?" he asked, batting his eyelashes at her.

"Annabel Park," she answered, obviously unfazed. Their hands detached, and she looked over at me. "I'd say that was a pretty good set."

"Good," I said. "Congrats again."

"Oh, Annabel, my darling," Ocelle crooned, holding out his arms, "you don't have to go just yet." She was grabbing her coat off the wall. "Please, stay. Sit next to us. Have a drink. Talk about the show."

Annabel looked between us uncertainly. "I don't know if that's a stellar idea. I've got to get home soon."

"A *stellar* idea? Well, why don't you sit right next to me, and I'll tell you all about this guy and his stellar ideas," Ocelle said.

That was what did it. Ten minutes later, we were all sitting together in the back room of Taylor's, waiting for Rigby to come and kick us out. We nursed Miller Lites and told stories. The air smelled of bread and rosewater, scents that wafted in from the kitchen. Annabel parted her hair down the front, her beer balanced between her legs, and began pulling out bobby pin after bobby pin. Ocelle, a little tipsy now, rubbed his eyes, creating even larger raccoon circles of eyeshadow that smudged down his cheeks like tear tracks.

"I'll tell you what we should do," he said, throwing his leg over the top of the couch and leaning back. "Let's start a band."

"A band," Annabel repeated, like the words were wholly unfamiliar.

Ocelle gestured to me with his beer hand. "Let's all be in this guy's band," he said, laughing. "What's it called? Mothic Wreckage?"

"I meant to ask. Is 'mothic' a word?" Annabel asked me.

I shrugged.

Ocelle sat forward, and a grin spread across his face, like he was at a campfire about to tell an epic story. His cheeks flushed, feverish, a bubblegum pink. "I'm telling you, it'd be a good band, too," he said. "You on the piano — sorry, the *guitar*," he corrected when I glared at him. "Annabel on the keys or the uke, then me on bass... now that's a winning trio."

To my surprise, Annabel laughed out loud. "There's no way I could ever be in a band," she said, speaking mostly to her beer can. "I'm always busy with work."

"So quit your job," Ocelle said. Like it was nothing. Annabel stared at him like he'd dropped from another planet.

"Anyways," I cut in, "I don't think Mothic Wreckage is a band. I don't know... *what* it is. A stage name, or something. Maybe just more of a concept. Whatever it is, I don't expect it to go far. It'd be stupid to waste all that energy on turning it into just another indie band."

Ocelle rolled his eyes and made a *blah blah blah* gesture with his hands, which made Annabel giggle. "God, Stars," he groaned. "You're just no fun, are you? Where's your sense of adventure? And excitement? C'mon, let's all start a band, and we can get outta here before that Rigby guy hires you as permanent in-house entertainment."

Annabel and I looked at each other uncertainly, then back at Ocelle, who waited with childlike eagerness.

That was the night the idea was born, and the next morning, I guess something Ocelle said had stuck with Annabel, because she called me, bright and early, at seven in the morning.

"Hello?" I asked blearily, rubbing sleep from my eyes and trying to adjust to the darkness of the room.

"Stars," she said, very officially, on the other end. "Mothic Wreckage should be a band. You, me, and Ocelle."

"Are you kidding? You've got to be kidding, right? Surely you understand the risks —"

"Stars." She cut me off, leaving no room for debate. "Mothic Wreckage should be our band."

I closed my eyes, warm in my queen bed. I only slept in one half of it these days. Under the comforter, my heart seemed to beat right out of my bare chest. I pictured Cal, a paintbrush in one of his calloused hands. He'd tell me to go for it. He'd tell me to write about him. I pictured it: me, Ocelle, and Annabel, all on a stage together, making our way around the world, writing music, and arguing over the meter. There was something so romantic about the idea, so aesthetically pleasing — and yet also something real. A chance to express myself. A chance to go around to all the places I knew and had yet to know and say *I love you. I will stay.*

Mothic Wreckage had been Cal's last gift to me, and now it was my gift to the rest of the world.

FOUR

It's been years. For a while, we were really good. We played a couple gigs and even landed a manager named Hazel, who managed to get us off the ground. We aren't The Strokes or anything, but we've made a name for ourselves. After Hazel quit (she couldn't stand Ocelle), we drifted along, half in purgatory. We were looking for a new member, a drummer, and eventually Kento fell into our laps. That was lucky. And now it's fine again: a year after this shifting ownership, we're on the road, playing to small — but well-attended — rooms. Four years down and an eternity to go.

In the van, Ocelle regales us all — me and the other band members, plus Therese, our photographer, and Stan, our new manager — with a tale from his youth. "There I was," he says, puffs of smoke shooting away from his face, "seventeen-and-a-half, dead on my feet, drunk in an empty Walmart parking lot. I turn around, and who is it that's driving towards me in a red Jeep? No one other than Maritza Kelsey, the prettiest cheerleader in school. I asked, 'Well, look who it is... what are you doing here?' and she said, 'Shut up, nerd.' So we had some fun together, and the next day at school, she acted like some fucking amnesiac."

No wonder, I thought bitterly, sipping hotel hot chocolate from my thermos. I'd seen pictures of Ocelle in high school, and he looked nothing like the lovingly-Freddie-Mercury-inspired person I knew today: short hair, braces, and a pimply, red face. He'd still had the same sense of humor, or so he'd claimed, but he had nowhere to go but up, appearance-wise.

It is remarkable to look over whilst on stage and see Ocelle next to me, playing the bass, commanding the crowd, demanding they fall in love with his beauty. I always get a little jealous. Ocelle knows everyone loves him, and he accepts it eagerly, feeding on their affections like a parasite. He never acts on his impulses to seize a beautiful person from the crowd by the hand, but it tempts him sometimes, I know. It would be hard not to fall in love with someone like Ocelle, someone who owns every inch of ground he steps on. Someone who throws his feather boas into the crowd. Someone who spends hours applying just the right amount of lipstick, then smearing it all in one big flush right before going out. That is Ocelle. My best friend.

As much as I love him and the other band members, things I can't tell them still linger in the forefront of my brain. It took me a while to open up to them about Cal, and even then I'm not sure that I really wanted to. None of them know my real name. That's one thing I'm determined not to give up, no matter how much they may want it; something has to give first, and I'm not going to incite it on purpose.

Ocelle laughs at his little story again and takes another hit. "Alright, Stars," he says. "Your turn. Give us something funny."

"A funny story?"

"Yeah. Can be anything. Just make it actually funny and not just, like, *Stars* funny."

"Ouch. Okay." I sit up in my seat and start to think. A funny story to tell? Hmm. Maybe the infamous Diet Coke incident (in which I, a sophomore in high school, managed to slam an entire liter of the shit in about two hours, and spent the remaining twenty-two hours of the day with my head stuck in a toilet)? Maybe the time Lily and I, drunk and wild, decided it would be funny to trespass and break into the neighbors' pool? Or perhaps the aftermath of that night when I went home and impulsively cleaned the whole house and fell asleep at the kitchen table?

Finally, the perfect story comes to my head. "I was really little," I preface. "I don't, um, talk to any of these people anymore. But still, it was funny."

"Shoot," Kento insists.

"I think I was only four or five. My oldest sister Violet got mad at me and Rosa for being annoying, I guess, so she locked us out of the house for a while. So Rosa went around the side to scare her, and Violet hit the window so hard it broke."

"No shit?" asks Annabel, as Ocelle starts to howl with laughter.

"Yeah. It was a big mess." I roll up my sleeve and show them my one souvenir from the incident: a small, jagged crescent moon of a scar just above my right elbow. "One of the glass shards hit me and did that, but I just remember laughing so hard about it."

Yes, I had laughed. As Violet and Rosa both cried and cried, my mom had come back and saw what had happened. My sisters were sobbing and fighting, but I was sitting on my butt in the grass, laughing, playing with a bloody shard of glass as easily as if it were my favorite toy airplane.

Whenever I think about being young, it is that memory that comes back first. My mom's scream of horror as she grabbed the glass out of my hand, gawking at the other tiny white sparkles like hints of snow on the concrete. My blood, an unfamiliar sight, and the new gash in my arm which seemed so big at the time.

I guess I say some of this out loud because the van becomes quiet and awkward. Everyone blinks at me. Ocelle yawns dramatically and stretches out, a lazy cat basking in the sun. Outside the windows of the van, the American country is fat and green under a cloudless sky.

—

We arrive in Salt Lake City later that night, eager to get some sleep and do some sightseeing in the morning. I'm still not sure if I'm going to be leaving the hotel much — I'm tired — but the others can't wait to go downtown. I'm becoming something of a wet blanket. Ocelle makes no secret of letting me know.

The hotel is a little less nice than what I had been expecting, not to sound stuck-up. There are two queen beds in our room, so Ocelle and I take one while Annabel takes the other; Kento, ever the gentleman, elects to sleep on the floor instead. The place is musty and smells of rot and age. Someone down the row is smoking; it reeks. Ocelle whips a little something out himself and grumbles when I tell him no.

After dinner, which is a DoorDash order from Taco Bell, we all sit on my and Ocelle's bed and watch Netflix on Kento's crusty old laptop. I'm so dead-tired I lean my head on Ocelle's shoulder, feeling his entire body stiffen. I don't know why, but it makes me nervous, even as he laughs along with Kento and Annabel.

I suppose, oddly, something about Ocelle has always made me nervous. I don't know what it is or where it is coming from. Something tells me it is not very important to figure out.

The next day, the show goes great — the air conditioning cuts out halfway through, so a groupie runs over to the convenience store and buys a bunch of water guns that we squirt into the crowd. The whole thing looks ridiculous, but it ends up being a lot of fun.

While we are waiting for the encore cheers to keep rising, Ocelle takes a hit from Kento's bong and turns to me with a winning smile. "Well, another one for the books," he says proudly. He is dressed like a ghost in white chiffon. "It's only uphill from here, Estrella."

"Don't call me Estrella."

Ocelle shrugs and sets Kento's bong back on the green room coffee table. "Everybody ready?"

"One second," Annabel grumbles, her phone pressed to her ear. She's been fighting on and off with her boyfriend Chris all day, about what none of us are sure. She mutters some blasphemies on her end and hangs up like she doesn't have a care in the world. "Alright, let's do it."

We head onstage, back in front of the cheering crowd. I lean towards the microphone and say, "Fine, you get us back," which raises the decibel level by quite a bit. I repeatedly fix the plastic orange earpiece that keeps falling onto my shoulder.

We end with "Castle of Girls" — no longer a sweet little romantic guitar ballad, but a classic rock-sounding story kind of song. The narrator asks us to imagine an infinite house of girls, one that stretches into some kind of never-ending hallway cluttered with games of cards and vanities and costume racks. There are all kinds of girls there. There are pretty blonde girls with cherry-red lipstick and blue sequined bras, brown-eyed girls that smell like coffee and hug you around your stomach when you wake in the morning, and redheads that read out loud and make your heart pound right out of its chest. But even with all these girls, these hundreds and thousands and millions of girls, he'd still pick you.

Cal and I wrote that together about a million years ago. He'd been painting our neighbor, an old friend, creating rings of brown in her almond-shaped eyes, and he said, quite out of the blue, "There should be a song just about girls. It's a pretty word, you know. *Girl.* I'm sure someone would listen to that."

I looked at him from my spot on the bed, where I'd been reading. He sat by the window at his easel, the half-finished portrait's eyes looking wistfully toward our ceiling. The springtime sun streamed in through the curtains and hit Cal right in the face, turning him into an ethereal angel, but if he minded, he did not show it.

"Did you hear me?" he asked softly, not looking back at me. "Write a song about girls. A whole palace of girls."

I suppose now, looking back on it, he'd meant for me to take it in a different direction, but I couldn't let Cal take all the credit. It had to be my song too, in some way or another.

The last notes fade out, the concert is over, and the room explodes into hysteria. I reach down and grab some of the clawing, reaching hands — some adorned with bracelets, some with rings, some with chipped nail polish like Ocelle's, but most with the large black X that designates them as being younger than twenty-one.

I despise young people looking up to me. I am twenty-four. Why would I have any idea what I'm doing? Just because I get to nap in a van?

I look over and see Ocelle doing the same thing, saying his 'thank you, darling,'s to the crowd. He is wearing a billowing pink satin robe. His hair is still a wild curly blob. He'd probably be better off keeping it pinned behind him during shows but he'd never admit that. Annabel is saying her thank-yous from a distance, mostly just to her little cheering section off to the right. Kento waves frantically from behind us all at the drum set (I know without turning around). Some people in the crowd start cheering his name. I'm relieved another show is over; something twinges in my knee, though.

Backstage, I head to the bathroom — a lot nicer than the one where Greta and I had so briefly united — and splash myself in the face with some water. I leave my glasses on the edge of the sink and stare at myself through the fogged mirror. I should bleach my hair again; the natural light brown is beginning to peek through at the roots. I don't know if I'll be allowed to bleach it now, or if I'll have to wait until the tour is over. The latter would be unfortunate. It's not very appealing.

The door behind me swings open, and there's Ocelle, yawning. We make eye contact in the mirror.

"Oh, sorry," he says. "Didn't mean to intrude on your pampering. Carry on."

"Wait," I say hurriedly, not thinking. I turn around and lean against the sink basin. He looks at me like he does not trust me, eyeing me up and down. "Stay for a second."

When I say this he giggles and steps forward, folding his arms. "Okay," he says. "Whatever you want. What can I do for you?"

From this distance, I can see how tired he is. His eyes are droopy, with large bags underneath. He reeks of sweat, but I couldn't care less. The hair at the nape of his neck glistens.

"Hmm." He tilts his head at me. "You look so different without your glasses on, you know."

"You must have seen me without them a thousand times."

He reaches past me and grabs the glasses off the sink, turning them over in his hands and examining them. "It's a marvel how you see out of them on stage, they're so dirty," he mutters, reaching forward and grabbing the hem of my shirt. As he cleans the lenses with the fabric, I breathe in, afraid to tense any of my muscles.

Ocelle lets go of my shirt and puts my glasses back on my face. His fingers, warm, linger against my cheek.

"Good show tonight," he says with a good-natured smile, drawing his hand back. "Hope your voice is hanging in there."

"It's fine," I murmur, barely audible.

"I'll see you back at the hotel." When I nod, he does too; he kisses me on the cheek, bows as he did on stage, and leaves the bathroom.

—

Just before heading out to the stage door, I run headfirst into Lily, and the two of us go stumbling backward.

"Oh!" she exclaims, her hands on her head to keep her ribbons from falling out. "I'm so sorry, Stars."

"That's okay," I say, using the wall to straighten myself out again. "It's... well, it's good to see you. What are you doing here?"

Lily blushes, red as a strawberry, brushing some short brown hair behind her ear. Her eyes are bright and hopeful. "I wasn't planning on it," she says. "I came into town with my brother to see our uncle, he's not doing well. I found out you guys were playing here, totally by surprise, and decided to stop by. I was gonna text you, but..."

"...but you're here now," I finish, and pull her into a hug. She smells good, like cinnamon and sweet tea. "Who let you in?"

"Annabel," she says from somewhere on my shoulder. When I pull away, she is still blushing, her large chunky cardigan falling off her arms. "I hope that's alright."

"More than alright." I hold out my hand. "You want to come out to the stage door with me?"

She glances behind us at the door where the security guard, a buff man of fifty or so, waits. She looks back at me uncertainly, nervous. "Are you sure that's a good idea?" she asks. "Won't people start talking?"

I shrug. "Let them talk. It doesn't make anything true."

With this reassurance, she smiles, and our fingers interlace. The security guard opens the door for us. Annabel, Kento and Ocelle are already gone, so most of the crowd has died down, thinking I wasn't going to come out. The few dozen that stayed cheer at a volume impressive for such a small group.

I look at Lily. "Just smile and wave," I suggest. "They'll like you."

I am talking more to myself than I am to her.

"Stan warned you two to stop drinking," I say to my bandmates.

"Fucking Stan." Ocelle yawns. "He should know by now — we've got a problem with authority."

"Should I take my leave?" Lily asks. Her eyes are still a little red-rimmed. How much weed did she smoke? Still, I'm dimly amused; Lily sounds like a little Victorian debutante when she's tired. "I don't want to overstay my welcome."

"Take all the time you need getting ready," Annabel insists curtly. She's been up for the least amount of time but is already half-dressed, pulling on a cardigan over her tank top. I don't think she meant to sound quite so prim and upset, but Lily blinks, obviously startled. I think Annabel hides a gentle heart beneath a cross exterior, but sometimes that line blurs and she seems truly angry. At what, none of us are sure.

Before long, we're all dressed and somewhat presentable, and I am walking Lily downstairs to call her a cab back to her uncle's. She seems happy to be in the fresh air again. She and I are still friends, undoubtedly, but something about us is awkward. I suppose that's just how it goes after you lose yourself to someone. You can't ever pick up the pieces.

"It's been really good to see you again," Lily says, not looking at me. "I'm happy for you."

"Thanks."

"Yeah." She scratches a blushing cheek with her pointer finger, which bears a small ring I gave her as a graduation present. It is shaped like a wolf. "I mean, I wasn't gonna say anything, but you guys look so cute together."

"Wait. Wait." I stop her where we're walking, right near the doors to the lobby. "What are you talking about?"

She looks at me sideways. "You and Ocelle," she says. "You're a thing now, right?"

"What are you talking about?" I ask, bewildered. "No. No way. Ocelle and I aren't a thing at all."

Lily blinks. Her little freckled face reminds me of a squirrel's, stunned and caught off-guard. "Oh," she murmurs, shifting her balance. "I thought... since you guys act so close and everything."

"Lily," I enunciate. "Ocelle is my best friend."

"I know, but I just thought —"

"No." I cut her off, firm and definitive. "Whatever you thought, you thought wrong. Alright? Ocelle and I aren't anything. We will *never* be *anything*."

I think the words come out harsher than I meant them to. Lily takes a little step backward, and before I know it, her eyes are lined with tears. "Okay," she says softly, wiping at the corners to preserve her mascara. "Sorry."

Feeling even worse than before, I hobble through the doors and call a cab for the sniffling Lily trailing behind. I sit with her in sticky lobby chairs and wait for the taxi to appear outside amidst the sedans and sports cars, and when it does, I walk her out again. It's started to sprinkle.

Lily opens the cab door, but before she does, she turns to me expectantly.

"I didn't mean to make you cry," I say, reaching for her hand. "I just... I don't know. Ever since Cal..."

"I know," she finishes for me. "I'm sorry I jumped to conclusions. It won't happen again." Thunder grumbles off in the distance as she pulls me into a hug, her cinnamon and tea smell mixing with the jasmine of the street air. "I'll see you soon," she promises. "I'll try and catch another show whenever I can, alright?"

"Okay."

She moves away from me, gives me a watery smile, and ducks into the taxi. I wave her off and wait until she's disappeared down the block before I turn and make the long, achy trek back to the hotel room.

perience. There aren't many hotels around here, he says, at least none in our budget. Ocelle and I look out of the windows as we pass each RV, kids running around with bubble wands and dogs barking at barbecuing men and fatigued wives emerging from trailers. Potted succulents sit in windows. The air is smoky and warm, but not unpleasant. The last few minutes of sunlight peer at us through the trees, so tall they could be redwoods — I wouldn't know the difference.

When we park in our spot, Ocelle and Kento tumble out and toss a frisbee back and forth. Annabel and Therese, our photographer, wander around, not doing much at all, and Stan stays inside the van to work on some emails. I tug on my knee brace — which I hope works — and head out to join the fun and games.

"You know something," Ocelle says as he holds up a pausing hand, bending to open the cooler and grab himself a drink, "this RV park thing isn't half bad. We ought to do this more often."

Kento laughs good-naturedly as Ocelle tosses the frisbee back to him. "Nah, it'd be too good for us," he says. "Stan likes to keep us humble. All those dank hotels."

I join the game, the three of us forming a triangle. Inside the van, I can see Stan, his face set with worry, the creases of his jowl lines deepening. Annabel and Therese have disappeared. Now that it's getting dark, the mosquitos are becoming more and more daring, and we find ourselves swatting at the air.

"Maybe I revoke my previous statement," Ocelle says with disgust, glaring at his arm, where a mosquito feasts. He smacks it quickly with his other hand, leaving only a splotch of blood where the pest had once been: the meal in progress. "What a fuss." He makes eye contact with me as he licks the red off of his wrist. "I'd prefer a hotel to this any day of the week."

"The mosquitoes don't bother me," Kento brags, his legs covered with welts and bites.

Ocelle and I just look at each other and laugh.

• • • •

Soon we discover how wrong we were to boast about our luxurious traveling conditions. We all pile back into the van once it's too cold to play frisbee anymore. We turn around the heater, which runs for about five minutes before sputtering out. Cold, and still in our clothes from the previous day, all of us — including Stan — huddle together in the back under one blanket, trying to stay warm. I am sandwiched between Ocelle and Kento, neither of whom is much good at sleeping in shared spaces, so I hardly get a wink all night. When the sun starts to come up just after five-thirty a.m., I straighten, grateful for an excuse to get out of the heap.

I look out at the sleepy RV park. I must be the only person awake in the entire world. The days end too soon and begin even sooner nowadays; there's never enough time to do anything.

Everyone else is sound asleep, tangles of limbs and hair under the threadbare little blanket. Ocelle is using Kento's chest as a pillow, and Kento's head leans against Stan's shoulder: some bizarre game of dominoes waiting to happen.

I shiver as I remember Cal, the way he'd wake with me around this time. I imagine the smell of sleep, his chest warm against my back as he pulled me under the covers with him. *Five more minutes.* Sometimes he'd whine that I worked too hard, and he'd yank me back with a little more ferocity, humming a song I didn't know.

Cursing myself, I curl back up in the crook of Ocelle's arm and close my eyes.

SEVEN

The show is subpar, to say the least. I don't think the audience notices any particular dip in quality, but I do, and the rest of the band does, too. Must have been something about sleeping in a rainy RV park, all piled on top of each other for warmth once the heating gave up on us. By the end of the encore break, all four of us are cranky and tired and sweaty, shoving and muttering to each other as we head out to the back door.

Of course — because that's just our luck — there's a small crowd of teenagers who have come to see us in action, and we spend a few minutes taking pictures, thanking people for coming out to the show, trying to ignore how fucking tired we are.

There's one girl who must be only eleven or twelve. When I am in front of her at the barricade, she looks at me with blushing cheeks.

"I've loved you guys for two years," she says sheepishly. "Do you think I..." She gulps. "D'you think I could get a picture with you?"

"For sure," I tell her, and I plaster on my usual post-show smile until she's satisfied and she and her mom have stolen away.

Sometimes I feel like an impostor. Part of me yearns to call back to that little girl, who was too young to be our fan by far; I want to tell her to pick something else. I want to apologize to her and her mom both. They didn't pay to meet me or anything (that's even worse) but I can't help but be entirely consumed with guilt. I watch their backs recede into the darkness across the parking lot while, next to me, Ocelle laughs dashingly and chatters with a young man as if they've been friends all their lives. I hate him when he is so badass.

. . . .

Later that night we arrive at our hotel, which is just past the state line.

"It's a different situation tonight," Stan says, as he grabs Annabel's luggage out of the back and hands it to her. "Managed to nab Annabel and Therese a room, and you three boys have to share."

"Really?" Annabel asks, slinging her bag over her shoulder. Therese heads over and stands next to her, smiling from ear to ear. They've become good friends recently. "You mean Kento's not gonna keep me up all night with his snoring? What a dream."

"Hey," Kento protests.

I look around and breathe in. The sky is dark and the wind is brisk. The lights of the Marco Hotel are on across the parking lot, but beyond it, few blazing centers of activity are alight. A farmhouse here, a convenience store there. As I have come to understand it, most of America looks the same. I believe they have a term for that. What is it... placelessness?

The hotel room is small. There are two beds, and the three of us look at each other, uncertain who will be the one to luck out. Ocelle doesn't stay bothered for long, though.

"We'll figure it out," he says carelessly, yawning and flopping over onto one of them. He fishes in the bedside cabinet for the TV remote. "Let's see if good old Mayim Bialik has followed us here."

Sure enough: *introducing today's contestants... a software engineer from Tampa, Florida...*

"Yes!" Ocelle exclaims gleefully, voice filled with childlike wonder. "Kento, we're eating good tonight."

Kento hops onto the bed next to him and watches the screen with newfound, rapt attention. I head into the bathroom, which is nicer than the one in Salt Lake, and check my knee. It looks a little swollen — purple and yellow, a rainbow missing vital shades — but it feels the same as it did this morning and last night. I run some sink water through my hair and brush my teeth (which desperately needed to be done). When I look in the mirror, I don't quite recognize myself.

"Stars!" Ocelle calls from outside the bathroom. "Come out here."

"In a second," I say. I hear his footsteps receding.

My face doesn't look like my face. If you asked me, "Oh, what does Stars Mainquist look like?" I wouldn't be able to tell you. I'd give you the general idea — my eyes are blue, and I dye my hair a lot, especially during crises — but you can't see me in your brain any more than I can. Sometimes I feel like a ghost, or a mirage, maybe. Anything you cannot see unless you stare directly at it, and even then the image is fuzzy.

When I leave the bathroom and re-emerge, I see Ocelle, his favorite little mirror balancing on his lap and a rolled-up twenty in his hand. Kento is sitting adjacent to him, and they both look at me, wide-eyed, like I've caught them in an act.

"Well, welcome back," Ocelle says. "Would you care to join us?" As if it's a fucking Victorian tea party.

"I'll pass," I mumble, and wobble over to the other bed to sit. I watch Ocelle get high off his supply, and then Kento follows suit. On *Jeopardy!* the Tampa software engineer is in the red, and he sweats visibly, his hand practically trembling with the buzzer.

The overhead lights are off. The clock on the wall says it's ten past eleven. A lipstick has fallen onto the floor; I can see from here that it is Ocelle's, matte and nude in color. I don't bother to pick it up. The lamp between the beds is dim, barely functioning, but cozy all the same. I nestle further into my jacket, finally getting into a spot where my knee isn't killing me, and close my eyes, listening to Ocelle and Kento's sniffing and giggling.

I must have fallen asleep. The next thing I know, I am awake, and Ocelle and Kento are screaming at each other.

"No, you're *always* fucking doing this shit!" Kento roars, pointing an accusatory finger at him. He's shirtless, heading back towards the door. "Don't act like you're so high and mighty when you don't even know your limits."

"The hell are you talking about?" Ocelle counters. He comes towards Kento, who keeps stepping back. "The *hell* are you talking about, Kento? When I know I need to stop, I fucking stop."

"Like hell, you stop!" Kento wipes his mouth with the back of his hand. "Are you ever *not* high? Do you ever fucking worry about yourself?"

"Oh, get off your high horse. You've been doing this shit with me all night long."

"Not as much as you have!" Kento points past him to the mirror, still dusty with white specks. "You always do too much! You get *crazy*!"

Ocelle folds his arms and glares at him. It startles me such that it fully rouses me from my sleep. I have never seen Ocelle look at anyone with anything less than neutrality, much less this level of hostility.

"I just worry about you, Ocelle," Kento says, his voice quivering. "I'm fucking *worried* about you. I'm saying this shit to you because I love you."

Ocelle doesn't answer. His hardened gaze does not leave Kento's face for a second.

Kento angrily rubs at his eyes and turns away. "Fine," he grumbles. "I'm going to sleep in the van tonight. Goodnight, Ocelle."

Nothing.

"I said goodnight, Ocelle."

"Go fuck yourself," Ocelle says.

Kento slams the door behind him. Ocelle wrings his hands and breathes hard, and then glances over to see me. He blinks in surprise. "Starry Night," he says. "How long have you been awake?"

"Long enough," I say, standing and going to meet him. "You want to tell me what that was all about?"

He laughs good-naturedly. "Just a little man-to-man talk, you know how it is. Nothing to worry about. Really."

Outside in the hallway, I can hear curious doors opening. Someone asks, "Man, who was that screaming?" Someone else, a woman this time: "I hope everything's okay."

Ocelle rolls his eyes. "It's like no one remembers how to mind their own business," he mumbles, dragging his hands down his face dramatically. "I mean, how hard is it to keep your door shut, your mouth closed, and sleep till the morning? Private affairs are just that — private. I don't understand why I should have to tiptoe —" He waves his hand around, and it is at this moment that his sleeve falls, and I see something that alters the course of both of our lives forever.

I make a wild grasp for his wrist, desperate to prove myself wrong, that it had only been a trick of the light. He wrestles away from me, but not fast enough, not before I see them: the bruises, purple and yellow and green just like my knee, kissing the inside of his forearm.

"Ah, yes," he says airily, prying himself out of my grasp like it's nothing. He shoves his sleeve back down. "Must've hurt it onstage or something. You know me, I can't stop fucking up like that. Right?" He laughs jovially and without fear or anguish, which sends a wave of nausea crashing over me.

"Look at me, Ocelle," I beg, my voice suddenly quite full of seriousness. I notice I am trembling. My head swims like I'm going to faint. "I said *look at me*."

He does, and the joking smile slides off his face. Perhaps it was never quite there to begin with, merely oil on water.

I breathe. Ocelle smells comforting, he smells like home. I want him. I don't know why or how or in what way, but I want Ocelle more than I've ever wanted anyone else in my entire life, maybe even Cal. "Please." My voice is now barely more than a whisper, harsh in my throat. My eyes blur with tears. "What's happening to you?"

He doesn't look me in the eyes. He only sits on the bed, his hands in his lap, fingers interlacing. In the light, he seems much older than before, and I wish he were asleep again. I sit across from him and lean forward, waiting.

"It's nothing." His voice is light, casual, but his facial expression is grave and grim. "Just a way to relieve some tension before the shows, that's all." His brown eyes find mine. His are so dark that it is hard to tell where his irises end and where his pupils begin.

I hold out my hands to them. "Do you mind if I take a look?" I ask softly. When he grimaces, I continue. "Only to look. Not to judge. Just to... get a better understanding."

Halfheartedly, he reaches his hands over and slides them into mine. His fingers are warm, and the soft cotton sleeves of his sweatshirt seem a cruel contrast to the topic at hand. Gently, I pull them back and look at the bruises again. They are not just on one arm, but both, making an odd pattern like an argyle. I let my palm rest over a particularly large one just underneath his wrist, appalled.

"I can't believe you would do this to yourself," I murmur.

He laughs and shakes his head. "Me neither."

"How long?"

"Oh, too long," he says with a shrug. "Since before we set off, even. Back during those first few weeks of rehearsal."

"And Kento knew but I didn't."

Ocelle shakes his head. "Not until tonight. I get a little loose-lipped sometimes when it's late. You know." It's true, I do know. Once we were up late drinking in my apartment and he told me, with multiple camera angles and perspectives, all about his first time on acid.

"I have to get you some help," I say softly, tracing an absentminded circle around another bruise that looks like a shooting star. "I can't let you keep doing this to yourself."

"Oh, don't worry about me." He yawns like he has a million more important places to be, and things to be doing. "I'll be fine. After the tour ends, I'll probably head back to my parents' place and get a job somewhere."

Behind me, I hear Ocelle sit up. "Oh, my," he says, yawning. "*I had the most marvelous dream, everyone. I had a dream Kento finally learned how to mind his own fucking business.*"

Sigh. The things being trapped in a van together will do to certain people, I suppose. Ocelle and Kento, at least, have turned into two boys out of William Golding. It occurs to me Annabel doesn't yet know what happened last night, so the tense silence must not be so palpable for her. For me, for Ocelle, for Kento, it is so thick I doubt you could slice through it with a knife.

—

The venue is a dingy one, to say the least. It is a tiny bar called The Borns, mostly standing room except for a few moth-eaten sofas in the corner. The cocktails are named after our songs, and Kento and I decide to try the "Castle of Girls" one, just for fun, but it tastes horrible: a violently sour concoction of lime, pineapple, and passionfruit. During the sound check, Ocelle turns to squint at me, tenting his eyes from the harsh lights. "Jesus," he mutters. "I never thought I'd enter a place I hated more than Rigby's, but here we are."

"You're mic'd," Annabel reminds him curtly, passing her ukulele pick between her spindly fingers.

We're in Nevada right now, so naturally, it's hot. I have a stool set up just in front of Kento's drum set a little way, waiting patiently and stacked with water bottles. Stan or someone can always run out and get more. I only hope it ends up being sufficient.

"I'm excited for tonight," I overhear the owner of the bar, a young guy named Jerry, say. I look over to see him leaning against the end of the bar, running a hand through fine ginger hair. "Haven't had this popular a band in, well, ever."

The bartender nods, looking pleased as she jots notes with a mechanical pencil. Later I'll learn she's Jerry's wife. "I know," she says. "Only up from here."

Only up from here. What an optimistic thing to say, one that Ocelle has said to me plenty of times. I look at him again, tuning his guitar. The bruises do not appear from underneath his tightly buttoned sleeves, but I know they're there. They stand out to me even when unseen, and my entire body boils with hate for them. I want nothing more than to gather Ocelle up, take him outside, and sit with him in front of the water or beneath a tree in the dark. There has to be more to life than a guitar and fights on a tour van and needles at three in the morning.

Therese appears on the other side of the stage, her camera around her neck, her face small and deerlike. "Hey," she mumbles, mostly to Annabel, "there's some talk that after the show we all might go and smoke a couple of joints at Jerry and Amber's apartment. If you guys are interested."

Annabel shrugs. "I don't know. I'll think about it."

I look around. Ocelle and Kento don't look at each other. Kento purses his lips.

"I'll pass," I tell Therese. "I appreciate the offer, but Ocelle has some music he wanted me to help him with tonight." I suddenly feel Ocelle whip around to gape at me, going from startled to exasperated to angry in a millisecond.

"Bummer," Therese says, and then turns to Kento. "What about you, Kento? It could be fun."

Kento's angry gaze remains fixed on the stage floor. The muscles in his thin jaw ripple. "Yes," he says tersely. "Yes, I will be able to go."

The set ends up being fantastic. About halfway through, the AC falters, so I and Kento both peel off our shirts. I'm rarely a shirtless-on-stage kind of guy, but sometimes it just gets too warm. We get Stan to go out and buy some more water, and we toss bottles into the crowd. The entire room reeks of body odor. Annabel and Ocelle are both sweating uncontrollably, wiping their foreheads with their sleeves. I feel myself burning — not only because of the temperature, but with pity.

NINE

A fter the next show, I'm walking past the crowd, which waits, pressed up against the barricades. Towards the back there's a very pretty girl: brown hair with a blonde money piece, blue eyes that seem to bore right through me. She sees me looking. I watch as she scans me up and down, less a fan and more a judge, and I gesture with a slight tilt of my head.

It's not long after that. The bathroom is a good hiding spot, and she's a good girl. She's on her knees in front of me and I'm staring at the little advertisement clipped to the inside of the stall door. Mothic Wreckage. One night only.

I hitch my breath, and she comes back up for air, smiling at me, as if to say, *Are you having fun yet?*

"That was great," I stammer. "Uh... thanks."

"No problem."

"What was your name again?"

She giggles. She reminds me so much of Greta. Of Piper. "Suki."

"Thanks, Suki." I reach past her and fumble for the door latch.

Suki pouts. "You're not gonna stay?"

"I can't," I lie. Quickly I redo my zipper (it would have been tragic if I'd forgotten that step) and step past her, towards the sinks. "But thanks, really," I say. "You're... you're really pretty."

She smiles, but I can tell she's disappointed.

I wash up and hail a taxi back to the hotel, where Kento and Ocelle — fucking of *course* — are screaming at each other.

They don't even look at me when I enter the room. Kento's talking, gesturing wildly: "You *kissed* Dunya?!"

"She wanted it!" Ocelle insists. "It had nothing to do with me."

"It had *everything* to do with you, you piece of shit. Keep your fucking hands off my girlfriend!"

"Whoa," I say, raising a hand. "Let's all take a second and —"

"Fuck off, Stars," Kento growls, turning to look at me. "Where the hell have you even been? Off fucking another fan?"

"You could use a more polite word, but yeah."

He rolls his eyes and turns back around to Ocelle, jabbing a finger in his face. "You ruined everything. She'd driven all the way out here, she... Dunya was *so* excited for the show and the afterparty."

"Yeah, really excited," Ocelle says.

Kento smacks him.

I sigh. I'm not even surprised anymore. I get into one of the beds and close my eyes, listening to their squabble continue.

"I just can't believe you would do that to me, Ocelle," Kento is saying.

"I can't believe you would do that to *me*," Ocelle responds, sounding hurt. "You *hit* me."

"You deserved it."

I somehow fall asleep to this.

Sometimes I forget their distaste for one another, but it always comes back to bite me. A snake right in front of me that I have been turning away from. They're both such stubborn, opinionated men. It's no wonder they butt heads. Even so, it doesn't exactly make my life (or relationships with each of them, for that matter) a walk in the park.

It wasn't always this way. Often I can close my eyes and imagine one of our first ever rehearsals as a group, before the bitterness had sweltered between them. It is three in the morning, and Annabel and I are in bean bags on Kento's apartment floor. She's asleep, curled up with her head against my thigh. Kento and Ocelle, though, are awake; Kento's on the loveseat, and Ocelle's sitting at the desk, and they are both a little drunk. Kento reaches out his hand in the yellowy lamplight. Sleepily, Ocelle smiles and touches the tips of Kento's fingers.

I think of that the next morning on the way to the next city. How inconsequential it was. How it'll never happen again, how we're all so far gone. We've become shadows of ourselves on this tour, I suppose, a

Therese head in first, but there's an arcade next door Kento wants to check out, so he lags a little behind. Ocelle also wants to see the arcade, and Kento doesn't object, so we send them off together. I imagine they look like two little fighting brothers in there, playing silent games of pinball side by side with jaws clenched and knuckles white on the knobs.

Annabel and I stand outside in the parking lot alone. The top of her head comes to about the height of my heart. Across the lot, the lights from the diner glow dimly, and I can hear the ping-ping-ping of an arcade machine. The sun has gone down, revealing a rural sky full of stars.

Annabel takes out a cigarette and a lighter. "Fuck, Stars," she says dryly, wiping smithers of ash off the shoulders of her leather jacket. "This is it, huh."

"Yeah. This is it."

I watch as she takes a hit. Then she passes it to me, and I do the same. I've never liked smoking, but fuck it. Since everything else about my life is changing, why not this, too?

"What am I going to do?" Annabel asks, her chin pointed at the sky. "Try and find Lily? Do something new entirely?"

"You could keep going," I say. "Everyone loves you. They'd follow you if you decided to go solo."

She shakes her head, and with a sinking feeling in my stomach, I realize her eyes are lined with tears. "No." Her voice is small. "I can't do that. I can't do this without you guys."

"You managed for a long time before you met any of us."

"Yeah, well, I'm never going back," she grumbles, plucking the cigarette out of my hand and wiping her eyes. "I can't believe we're arguing over this. It's not fair. My whole career is about to fall apart just because of a couple of fucking boys."

"I know. I —"

"You too!" she says. She jabs an accusatory finger in my face. "Don't you remember? You opened for me. You showed me up in front of *everyone*. I told you openers weren't supposed to be that good. I let you get into my head, and Ocelle started talking about making a band, and I..." She blinks. "Fuck. What have we done?"

She throws her cigarette on the ground and crunches it under an angry boot. She folds her arms and begins to pace in front of me, the diner illuminating different parts of her face as she turns. "I didn't even know you people. I didn't know you at all. And I let you turn me into this... this *thing*. All of us just turned into monsters. We all started hating each other, and I just let it happen."

"It's not your fault, Annabel." I stop her by placing a hand on her shoulder, and she looks at me venomously. "You're right. It's mine. Maybe it would have been better for everyone if Mothic Wreckage had just... never been."

As soon as I say it, I feel all glimpses of Cal leave the world. Every street corner is now just another street corner, the lamplights are no longer works of art, and the world tells me no more love or light or laughter is to be seen or heard or had.

I am destroying the last little bit of him I had gotten to keep, the piece that I had sworn to keep and protect.

"Annabel," I murmur, my voice now soft, buzzing with smoke, "I think Cal would be really, really upset with me."

She shakes her head. "It's not just about Cal anymore, Stars."

"But still. He'd hate the way things turned out. This is what he wanted more than anything in the world."

She arches a doubtful eyebrow at me.

"Do you want to hear a story?" I ask her.

"What kind of story?"

"A Cal story."

She hesitates, but I see her come around. She gives me a curt, almost indistinguishable nod.

I reach for the key to the van, hidden in my back pocket, and click the button to unlock it. As the doors slide open, I hop into the back, holding out my hand for Annabel to take.

ELEVEN

I rush into the living room, where Cal is on his knees in the kitchen, struggling for the edge of the counter. He laughs, easygoing and happy, but next to him on the floor is an overturned muffin tray. The batter has splattered everywhere. There's a dish towel that has fallen, too. A bruise is breaking out on Cal's elbow, large and ugly and unkind.

"Are you okay?" I ask him, rushing to help him up.

"I'm okay," he assures me. He leans on me for support. "It's a wonder I wasn't hurt worse, you know, I slipped quite dramatically. Shame about the muffins, though... mmm. Swings and roundabouts."

I lead him over to the couch, where he curls up and nestles his head against my shoulder. I grab his arm and turn it over in my embrace, studying the wounds. Blood rises to the skin. He must have scraped something on his way down.

"I'm fine," Cal promises easily. "You know, it's not the worst thing that's happened to us recently. Stop worrying. You're like an old mother hen."

"Whatever. I'm just concerned about you."

He looks up and kisses me. "Well, stop."

As if I ever could.

"So." He leans out of my embrace and sits, proud and tall, on the other end of the sofa, some sort of bruised king. He grabs a lollipop out of our jar, unwraps it, and settles back against the cushion. "Are we going to talk about Mothic Wreckage, or not?"

"Not this again."

"Yes, this again!" he exclaims, pushing me playfully on the shoulder. "I love the idea. I love the name. *Mothic Wreckage*. You know, if you don't make it into something, I'll probably never forgive you."

"Ouch."

Cal laughs and leans over again, settling his head in my lap. The lollipop stick looks like a cigarette. He is lighter than he was this time

That is how Ocelle comes to live with me.

Maybe you think I am foolish for letting him. And maybe I am. But I'm truthfully sick of coming home to the empty apartment, remnants of Cal strewn around like stray leaves: sweaters balled up in corners, paintings on the walls, the pillbox I didn't know what to do with afterward, books filled with doodles, the mixtape he made me for Christmas one year. The can of the last ever Daytime Watermelon Burst he had, sitting on my bedroom windowsill, glinting in the sun while the windchimes we made on his twentieth birthday tinkle above. A vase of dead Californian poppies — one of Rigby's little pity presents. These objects, remnants of a long-forgotten past, are irreversible tornadoes, and they eat at my heart.

It's not like Ocelle has never been inside my apartment before, but when we step inside, he looks at it in awe, like it's brand spanking new. To be fair, I do have a nice place. The windows are large, with lots of sunlight cascading over the hardwood floors. Cal's art decorates the walls. It's not a much-lived-in space, but it's nice, and it's good enough for me. It'd be a lot less decorated had Cal not been smart while he was alive. He always seemed to know what colors should go where in this place: pink and green behind the sofa, blue and yellow in the hallway. It is like having him watch over me, still. The first time Ocelle came over, he'd pointed to one of the canvases I had yet to hang and said, "Did you do that? Wow, it's really good for a Stars Mainquist original."

Bristling, I'd said, "Cal made that one." I had told him about Cal not too long prior.

"...oh."

Now, Ocelle immediately flops over onto my couch and makes himself at home. "Now this is what I call luxury," he says loftily. "Glad to be back in this haven instead of that shithole van."

I set our bags by the door — I'll unpack later — and head into the kitchen. My fridge is empty, except for a couple of things my housesitter must have kept for herself. A half-eaten bag of stale chips is on the counter. "We'll order in," I decide, standing again. "What do you want?"

"I dunno. I'm fine with whatever." I hear a click and some new buzzing voices. Ocelle has turned on the TV. One of his favorite sitcoms, *Bad Habits*, is on.

A half-hour later, we're still waiting on the pizza from Nick's. Slowest delivery of all time, I'm willing to bet. Kento and Annabel are both probably ordering from them, too, so they remain our playful competitors even post-tour. The thought is amusing but quickly rots and sours. *Mothic Wreckage*. Now that we are home, in less-than-ideal circumstances, what will happen to Mothic Wreckage?

I suppose nothing will fall apart in the Yeats way I am imagining. We have other things to do. After Ocelle recovers, and I can hopefully help him wrestle himself away from all those substances, we'll revisit it. Maybe it's not a goodbye, just a see you later. I can patch everything up between Ocelle and Kento, we can get back to work on recording our next album (which was what we were doing before the tour), and everything will be okay again. That's the game plan, I assure myself. Stars always has a game plan.

"You're worried about the band," Ocelle guesses, studying me.

"Is it so obvious?"

He smiles wide. He looks quite different when he isn't wearing eyeshadow and when his hair is pulled into a sloppy ponytail like now. "You make this face whenever you're thinking about something stressful," he teases. "You look like this." He scrunched his eyebrows and scowled.

"Guilty. Do I really look like that?"

"Stop worrying," Ocelle says, ignoring my question. He reaches over and tousles my hair. "It's going to be okay, and none of it was your fault, blah blah blah. Now shut up, I think *Friends* is coming back on."

My phone buzzes in my pocket. I fish for it, thinking it's probably the pizza delivery driver asking for the gate code. Maybe Lily, seeing when she can come over and visit us. But no, it's neither — it's my mother.

Fuck.

"Who is it?" Ocelle asks, craning his neck to see.

"The devil," I answer. And I, cursing myself, head back into the bedroom to pick up.

My mother is the most complicated person I know, beyond even Ocelle or Cal, and I doubt I would be able to explain her if I tried. Piper liked her, which maybe says more about Piper than anyone else.

"Stars," she says breathlessly into the phone when I answer. She calls me by my actual name, but I don't like that, so I pretend she says *Stars*. "I've been so worried about you. You haven't called me since before the tour started, I haven't heard a word from you in *months* — and then I hear your band is just, what, *over*? Done with?"

"I texted you," is my defensive little answer.

"You know that's not the same."

"Whatever." I scratch my cheek. "I've been busy."

I hear her make a whimpering noise. "Are you okay?" she asks softly. "I mean, really?"

"I'm fine."

"Are you back home again? Is anyone with you? Can I come to see you?"

"I'm home again," I say, instinctively holding up a hand without really realizing she can't see it. "I have Ocelle with me, he'll be with me for... I don't know how long. But it's probably not a good time."

Ocelle likes my mom alright. He finds her pitiable in a funny kind of way. I don't think he'd mind if she came over, but the truth is, if I opened the door and saw her standing there with those misty eyes, her hands pressed over her heart, I think I'd just die.

"Let's get together sometime this week," Mom pleads. "I want to see you — I *need* to see you."

There's nothing left in my soul anymore except for pity when it comes to my mother. "Fine," I say, mostly to ease her. "I'll text you, okay?"

• • • •

The pizza eventually does come, along with two Cokes. Ocelle and I sit side by side, eating equal halves of it and watching some kids' cartoons. I really should cancel cable TV; there is never anything good on. In the show, two characters sit in a school auditorium waiting for a show to begin, the air thick with silence. I wonder if that's what it looks like before we go out onstage. I made it a rule never to dare peer out at a crowd.

With a chill, I ask myself if this will be the rest of my life: catering to Ocelle, waiting for my mother to hang up the phone, stressing about Mothic Wreckage, looking over at Cal's paintings on the wall, and feeling myself want to shrivel up and blow away. That sounds worse than purgatory. I don't think I can do this. I don't think I want to do this, but then again, what choice do I have? What direction is there to go in except forward?

Ocelle yawns and leans his head on my shoulder. His hair tickles my neck, but I don't tell him to move.

"How do you feel?" he asks me.

"A little bummed, man. I'm not gonna lie."

"Yeah." He reaches over and shuts the pizza box with his foot. "You'll be alright. You've gotten through much worse than this, and so have I. You'll come up with some new ideas soon."

"I need to find work. I could go back to Conan's and see if they're hiring. Or maybe Rigby could use an extra hand at the bar, or —"

I cannot finish my sentence because Ocelle has turned my face towards his and kissed me square on the mouth, hard. And, as if I am signing my death certificate, my heart exploding in guilt, I do not pull away.

THIRTEEN

Cal and Ocelle would have liked each other. I think they would have been friends. They were more alike than they were different.

I think about that while Ocelle is getting ready for bed. I am sitting on the couch, writing some emails to Stan, and Ocelle is showering; I can hear him singing one of our songs. "Cherub, Mine." He's in the bathroom where I found Cal, which I hate because it's my only bathroom. I can't look at the tile floor without remembering the way the door had been left open. The dripping of the faucet.

And Cal looking up at me like a caged animal once I'd come rushing in — eyes brimming with tears, his lips dripping red — and saying, in his soft, fear-stricken voice: "*Stars.*"

It wasn't long after that.

Lily doesn't like to go into that bathroom either. It makes her cry. She wasn't even there but it makes her cry.

Speaking of Lily, she comes over for dinner a couple of days after the end of the tour. Annabel also joins in. It's been a long time since my dining table seated more than just one person at a time. The placemats are mismatched, and the vase in the middle is chipping around the rim, but the whole room is happy to entertain tonight.

I'm a fairly bad host. Cal always did all the talking. Lucky for me, Ocelle's akin to one of those fancy ladies on the *Titanic*, throwing around endless conversation topics easily. He charms Lily's socks right off, as usual, but Annabel, ever the same, only rolls her eyes every time he calls her his "darling love affair." He keeps the glasses well-filled with champagne and serves coffee with too much cream.

"Well." Ocelle clears his throat and holds up an old wine glass, the dregs of Pinot Noir sloshing around at the bottom. "A toast, then. To Mothic Wreckage, that old banshee, may she rest in peace."

Gingerly, I tap my glass against his. The air is bitter and acrid as if it is burning. Behind us, on the wall, is a pinned up poster from our first ever gig as a band, crumpled and lonely looking.

"Don't you think we could toast to something else?" Annabel asks, jaw set. "It doesn't feel right. Not when Kento's not here."

"Cheers to Kento's absence," Ocelle replies immediately, lightly touching the rim of Annabel's glass with the dimpled bottom of his own. "What a glorious occasion it is, truly. Doesn't the evening just reek of possibility?"

Lily stares at her half-eaten food. If Ocelle notices, he doesn't care, and he glugs the rest of his wine as easily as if it were water during an encore break.

I fidget in my seat. I've barely touched the spaghetti on my plate, even though I'm starving. The steam wafts up and out and into my face.

"Tell me," Ocelle says, not looking at any of us in particular, "what are you going to do now that our little club has dissipated?"

Annabel and I look at each other. "Who are you talking to?" I ask.

He seems not to have considered this. He's been running his finger in a circle on the tablecloth, but when I speak to him, he stops. "I guess I'm asking both of you," he says indifferently.

I shrug. Annabel does, too.

"I think it will be a long time before any of us knows what to do," she says. "The band was my lifeline. To think it's over, all because of you and Kento's fight —"

"Can we change the subject?" Lily asks abruptly. In the yellow light of the dining room, the pins in her hair glint and gleam. "I just... I don't like seeing you all so unhappy. Especially with each other."

"Anything for you." Ocelle reaches over and tops off her wine glass, filling it to a comical level. "What shall we talk about, then?"

Silence. I pick at a splotch of green paint on the table, left over from one of many of Cal's passionate pottery projects.

Annabel clears her throat. "Well, actually," she says, "that's another thing I wanted to tell you all about. I got a gig for this weekend. Finally, I can do something other than take naps all the time."

This catches everyone's attention, and we all look at her. She does not smile, but I watch as her cheeks redden with a familiar flush of pride. She sits a little straighter in her chair. "Up at the Temptation. This Saturday night. I'm opening for some kid, a senior at the high school, but still. I'm excited."

"They didn't have you as the main act?" I ask, astounded.

"They were going to." Annabel finishes off the last of her spaghetti, tainting her lips with the remnants of the tomato sauce. "But I told them I didn't want anything big. I'd either open for that kid or I was out."

Silence. Ocelle is gaping at Annabel, but Lily is still eating like this is no news to her.

"That's nice of you, Annabel," I say.

She shakes her head. "I didn't do it to be nice. I did it to preserve my sanity. I can't stand on a stage alone as the main act without the rest of Mothic Wreckage all around me."

The brief pauses of silence between our sentences are unbearably long and tense. Finally, Ocelle stands from his chair and appears behind Annabel, wrapping his arms around her shoulders in a warm, congratulatory embrace.

"That's lovely news," he says, kissing the top of her head. "We should celebrate, don't you think?"

• • • •

In the living room, Ocelle produces the goods, and we share them in a clockwise circle. I should tell you everyone else shares — I don't partake. Normally I would, but something about tonight has put a bad taste in my mouth. I sit on my ragged old couch under a fuzzy blanket, next to Lily, while Ocelle drapes himself over the armchair on the other end like some sort of deluded Aphrodite. Annabel is quiet when she is under the influence, and that's true now, too; she does nothing, says nothing, only occasionally takes a hit off the joint and looks straight ahead, clenching her jaw.

Lily leans her head on my shoulder. "That's better," she says, her voice mellow and kind. She's holding an amethyst geode, which Ocelle keeps on the table next to the couch, turning it over in her hands like it's magic. Her honey-brown eyes are dim from the weed. "I didn't like dinner much. We were all so tense with each other. It's better out here."

"Couldn't agree more," Ocelle responds airily, his throat pointed towards the ceiling. "To be fair, Stars' cooking would put anyone in a bad mood, hmm?"

I roll my eyes at him. He gives me a sideways grin.

"Annabel," Lily says, "we'll all have to get together and come watch your gig. I think that'd be a lot of fun."

"Yeah, when is it, again?" I ask.

"Saturday at seven. The Temptation."

Ocelle laughs. "You'd think they named it after the fucking group, right?" he asks. "The Temptations? What an uncreative name for a club. If I ever had one, I'd call it something much better."

I run through my mental calendar and cringe. My mother has asked me to meet her for dinner on Saturday night. "I don't know if I can go, Ann," I admit. "I might be busy."

She arches a singular sharp eyebrow at me. "Oh."

"I'm sorry. I'll see if I can reschedule it."

She doesn't say anything, and I know I've offended her. This is a conflict of interest: my mother, or Annabel.

The rest of the night is spent in relative discomfort. We turn on a horror movie after a while — it's not good, one of those straight-to-DVD things, since I don't have Netflix — and then Ocelle heads back into the kitchen to nab the bottle of Mephisto. He hasn't always been an absinthe guy, only more recently, and although he'd never admit it, it knocks him on his ass. He's the only one to drink it. In no time at all, he's truly crossfaded, twirling his copper keys around on his finger, yammering on and on about the Hedonistic age and the old teachers from his high school and all the various people he's kissed. It's entertaining, I suppose.

This continues well into the night. Annabel doesn't want to drive home, which I would have prohibited her from doing anyway, so I order her an Uber. I stand out in the cold on the curb, watching the girls load into the little red Toyota. If we weren't out here, it would be completely noiseless, utterly drained of life. Moths flicker under the lamps.

"See you on Saturday night, maybe," Lily says, pulling the car door open. "Love you, Stars."

"Love you too. Be safe."

I wait until they have disappeared before I turn and go back inside. Ocelle is still drinking, watching green liquid slosh around in his glass. When he sees me, he smiles. "Said *adieu* for the evening?" he guesses, his voice dripping with sarcasm. "Bummer."

I sit next to him on the edge of the couch, trying to make the least amount of contact possible. He is taking up the vast majority of the space, anyway. His sweatpants are worn, his socks filled with holes, his breath reeking of alcohol. Often, you'd think someone would change after knowing them for four years, but with Ocelle, not a thing has been out of place since the moment we met at Conan's. The same lace-up boots he'd been wearing on that very afternoon are in the kitchen right now, muddy, kissing the edge of the oven mat.

I glance at the clock below the TV. "It's past two," I say. "You should get some sleep."

"No." Ocelle holds the bottle close, peering into it. He laughs, hushed. "I'm not quite done."

"Come on, Ocelle." I hold out my hand and gesture for the absinthe.

He isn't happy about it, but eventually, I manage to wrestle it away from him and back into the cabinet. Once I do, feeling more than a little bit like a mother confiscating toys, Ocelle suddenly and dramatically complains he's oh so tired, and won't I please be a darling and help him to bed, and wouldn't I be so kind, blah blah blah.

My bedroom, ever since Ocelle moved in with me, has become a flurry of feather boas and glass beads. My bed is still mostly as it had been — threadbare sheets, an uninteresting comforter — but Ocelle brought with him a large and heavy orange quilt, which is strewn across the bottom of the bed. As far as I know, it's the only thing he would call a memento, as he offhandedly mentions it was his mother's a long while ago. Around the bed, there's hardly an inch of carpet that hasn't been covered by his clothes: velvet vests with gilded buttons, brown leather jackets with rips in the lining, his favorite shift. Perfume bottles sit on the bedside table. He hangs little sticky note drawings near the door, just so I'll see them when I head out in the mornings; they're not good, some are barely intelligible. But one I do laugh at is one of the two of us, in all our stick-figured glory, fighting over who gets the last beer in the fridge.

Tonight, though, I am not laughing. With Ocelle slumped over my shoulder, I push my way into the bedroom, dragging various articles of clothing out of the way. I finally manage to settle him on the bed, where he grabs my wrist and whines, "No, don't go quite yet." I watch, cautiously, as Ocelle scoots over and pats the space on the bed next to him. "Come sit."

I do. For a moment, neither of us says anything. The only light in the room is the lamp on what was Cal's half of the bed. On top of the covers, I am cold and solitary. Ocelle sprawls out on the pillows and yawns, but pops back up a moment later, his eyes glinting at me in the dark.

"My sister used to say something funny," he says, and I perk up instantly because this is new information. I barely know Ocelle as having a sister at all. "She used to tell me I looked like a disgraced English royal... cast out from the throne room and the gilded halls of Buckingham Palace."

I don't say anything. I don't know what to say.

But Ocelle continues, leaning over and grabbing my hand in the dark: "She always said I gave that impression of being someone important who was ousted from their usual place. She said I didn't deserve my birthright."

"I don't think she should have said that to you."

"You know what?" he asks, tauntingly. He grabs the gold chain of one of his necklaces and rests it atop his chin. "You know what *I* think? I think you should loosen up. You're very tense. I don't know if it's about the band, or what..."

"Of course it's about the band. What else is there to stress about?"

Ocelle laughs. He positions himself so he is now in front of me, one leg on either side of my lap. He rests his hands on my chest. "Stop worrying about it," he says, one finger tracing up my sternum. "All's well that ends well, or whatever."

"What are you doing?"

He shrugs. "You're just pretty right now. I dunno."

"Ocelle, you're not thinking clearly."

He gives me a playful pout and inches his face closer to mine until our noses are centimeters apart. He smiles cockily. "I never do," he brags. "That's what makes me so cool."

My chest bubbling with panic, I reach out and put my hands on his shoulders, gently pushing him away. "Ocelle," I insist, "you're not in your right mind. You can't consent. You don't want to do this with me, and I don't want to do this with you."

He reels back and hops off of me, folding his arms and turning away. He seems instantly sobered.

"It's not that I'm not flattered," I say, "but —"

"Oh, you're *flattered*, are you?" he asks, turning to glare at me with venom. "Well, haven't I just struck gold, then? Maybe you're right. I'm not in my right mind. Maybe I never was." He stands and drags himself into the bathroom, where I hear him turn the tap on.

I don't stay long after that. I head back to the couch, pull one of the worn old blankets around my shoulders, and try to sleep.

FOURTEEN

The next morning, Ocelle pretends last night didn't happen. I don't know if he remembers it or not, but I'm not about to ask. He greets me with his usual airy cheeriness when I wake — thanks to his clamoring of pots and pans in the kitchen, his humming of Mozart — and offers me some toast. Today I'm going to Conan's to ask for a job. I can't sit on my ass anymore, not if I want to keep supporting myself and Ocelle. I don't necessarily want to get evicted from my apartment, either.

"You'll get the job no problem," Ocelle says, tossing a tangerine my way. He is dressed in nothing but a silk slip, the thin straps falling off of his defined shoulders. "I mean, come on, the former frontman of Mothic *Wreck*age? They'd be a fool not to hire you. Hell, they'll probably slap your face on some posters. *Stars Mainquist Works at Conan's Now! Minimum Wage! Come buy your Gene Vincent from him! L'étoile n'est officiellement plus célèbre!*"

I try not to imagine this as I peel the tangerine, the smell erupting from it and mingling unpleasantly with the lavender scent of the living room. Ocelle finishes making his breakfast, which is just a couple of sausage links and a single hard-boiled egg, the last one. As he sits across from me, I begin my perfunctory and silent search for bruises and scratches on his bare arms — a now daily activity. Just to make sure all is well. There are a couple, few and fading, but they're there. No new ones. Not since last Friday.

Ocelle raises a glass of orange juice like he's toasting me. "Whenever you're in that little interview room," he says, "just think of me. Or just imagine everyone's in their underwear, or whatever they used to tell you about stage fright."

I have to laugh. My sisters used to pretend everyone was dressed like a banana. I am easily amused by little things.

My city is gray and cold, windy and sullen. I sit hunched over in my car's front seat and listen to the radio, where some Instagram mutual of mine croons about missed opportunities and missed trains. Out the windows, I watch the rain fall on kissing pedestrians and mothers with children in strollers. What do they call them in Britain — prams? That's a good word.

As we continue to get closer and closer to Conan's, the number of people I see along the streets wanes. A high school girl with scuffed-up knees in denim shorts walks to school here, a homeless man panhandles in fingerless gloves there — until, finally, no one remains, and I am alone in front of the ghost town that is Conan's Records.

It begins to rain.

Inside, it is just as it had been on the day I met Ocelle. It is just as charmingly filthy, just as lovingly disorganized. Matt Maltese and Buddy Holly sit on the same shelf. The sound of the rain pounding against the window does little to calm my mood.

At the counter is a young guy, maybe my age or a little younger, flipping halfheartedly through a magazine. He glances at me when I come in and blinks, clearly a little startled. His nametag says *Hi! My name is RAMIRO.*

For a moment, neither of us says anything to the other.

"The fuck?" he finally decides.

I sort of figured I'd get that sooner or later. I head over to the counter. He swipes the magazine into the floor.

"Hi," I say. It's as good a start as any. "I'm Stars, uh, and, well, I, uh —"

"Yeah, yeah, I know who you are," Ramiro mutters, his eyes narrowing. He has a freckly face, tan and blushing, his cheeks stained with surprise. "Who wouldn't? What the hell are you doing in here?"

I look around, not sure what to say. "Well," I start again, "I want to talk to someone about maybe getting a job here."

Ramiro looks at me like I dropped from the sky, which I may as well have. "A job," he repeats. "Here."

"Yes."

"Why?"

"It's a long story." I rub the back of my neck. "I just... is there anyone I can talk to about that? A manager, maybe?"

"Yeah, let me go get him," Ramiro says. He does a three-sixty and ends up right back where he started, only this time smiling charismatically at me. "Hi, I'm the manager," he warmly announces. "What can I do for you?"

"Well, I just told you. I need a job. Are you guys hiring?"

Ramiro rolls his eyes. "Are we ever," he says. "I don't know what anyone from Mothic Wreckage would want with a shithole like this, but employees are employees, y'know? I'm happy to discuss something with you."

"Great," I say, my entire body flushing with relief. For a minute I'd been scared he was going to turn me away altogether.

Forty-five minutes later, I'm an employee at Conan's, and Ramiro is explaining the rules as we walk the musty aisles. I'm not to mess with any of the Employees' Picks except for my own, which I won't get to select until the start of the next month. Juniper, the other employee, gets grouchy whenever anyone plays any Ink Spots, so that's off-limits on the jukebox. And a special rule, just for me: if anyone asks me, my name is Henry and I have never heard a single Mothic Wreckage song in my life.

"Why?" I ask Ramiro, following him into the next aisle over.

"I want people to buy music because they want to buy music," he says curtly. He doesn't look back at me. "Not because Stars Mainquist asked them to check out 'Cherub, Mine.'"

It's good enough for me. I'm a good liar.

• • • •

I don't hate working at Conan's as much as I'd figured I would. I come in every morning and say hello to Juniper and Ramiro, and I go about my business: selling people Britney Spears and Lesley Gore. Asking, "Who?" whenever someone brings up Stars Mainquist or Mothic Wreckage. Taking five-minute breaks at the top of every hour, just to go back into the breakroom and massage my temples a little bit, maybe steal an orange juice box from the minifridge and heat a sandwich for myself. Sometimes I browse the aisles just to browse, not to clean or sort, and on even rarer occasions I might find something I want for myself. Japanese Maple. Emiko Wakayoshi. Jumpscare Gender. I form an artillery using my thirty percent-off discount.

The days begin to run into each other. Ocelle gives me tarot readings, we go on walks around the apartment complex, exchange mischievous looks, and steal cigarettes from convenience stores.

Working at Conan's turns out to be the only thing I can think to do with my time. Kento and Annabel are also scrambling to find work, which means there isn't much time to even talk about recording the new album, much less Ocelle's level of involvement. I don't want Ocelle to have to worry about money, so I tell him not to find a job. He spends his time loitering around the apartment, hanging beaded curtains over the bare window in my bedroom and sketching from pictures he finds stuffed in my file cabinet. He tries to make friends but it doesn't work much of the time. His light brown hair continues to grow. I worry about him even when he's not looking.

I do keep my promise to my mother, as much as I might want to forget I ever made it. Annabel is not happy to hear I can't attend her gig at the Temptation, but I'm sure she'll get over it soon. I get off early from Conan's, throw my bag over my shoulder, and head out to my car. I drive Ocelle around a lot in the evenings, just to get him out of the house, so it's started to smell like him. Less like weed now, and more like perfume. As I turn the key in the ignition, I imagine he's next to me, leaning his head out the window like a dog.

My mother asked me to meet her at a place called Yndo, some sort of Asian fusion restaurant. I'd been a couple of times with the band, but I wasn't aware my mother knew it existed. I thought about what to say, what to do, and how to act the whole way to the place. My mom is an enigma and I don't quite know how to interact with her — I never have. Quite frankly I think she's insane.

I walk into Yndo and spot her immediately, a tiny shadow of a woman in a large booth towards the corner, completely alone. When she looks, she sees me, and her lips part. She seems to retreat even further unto herself as I sit.

For a minute, neither of us says anything.

"Hi," I eventually acquiesce.

"Hi." Her voice is even tinier than her body. I do not know how I was born from someone so incredibly meek. The only thing about her that is not small is her nose, which twitches nervously like some sort of rodent's.

"Why did you want to meet?" I ask her. "Be real about it. Don't just feed me a line about how long it's been."

She laces her fingers together on the table surface. Her little blue eyes are impossibly misty, even though I've only been sitting here for a minute or two. "Your entire life has changed since we last spoke face to face," she says quietly. "It's my job to keep up to date."

"Yeah, you've done a great job of that, haven't you," I mutter, leafing through the menu. "Mom, I will give you a million dollars if you can remember any of my bandmates' names."

She blinks. "Hold on," she says. "I'm thinking. There's the one with the long hair..." She gazes off into space, her hands clasped firmly, but before long, her shoulders sag and she sighs.

I'll keep my invisible fortune, then.

"I'm sorry," Mom murmurs. "I know it's on me. I know it is."

Yes. Everything is on you. From the first scoff to the latest misplaced call.

"I want things to be different between us," Mom says. "Better."

"It's gonna take a lot of work to make that happen, Mom."

"I know, I know, I know. But Stars — you're my only son and I *need* you. Like I need air."

I absentmindedly run my hand over the crescent moon scar on my arm. If my mother needs me like she needs air, I need her like I need a lobotomy. My entire body crawls with discomfort.

"Please give me a chance to make things work out." Without asking, she reaches over and takes my hand in hers. Her fingers are cold. "It would really and truly mean the world to me."

I think about what Cal would say: he'd tell me to stay. To make amends. He knew the horrors my mother had put me through, but Cal had always been annoyingly prone to forgiveness. He did not like to dislike people. He would jut his chin out defiantly and tell me no matter what anyone did, he loved them anyway, because on a fundamental level everyone was the same. (It used to eat at me.)

Ocelle would tell me to flip her off and leave as haughtily as I'd entered.

Instead, I elect to do neither. I gently wrestle my hands away from my mother's grasp and stand, pulling at the hem of my shirt. "I appreciate you trying to atone," I admit, "but I think it's too late. And I think you and I both know that."

"What am I supposed to do?" she asks, beseeching. "You never reach out. You never call. How am I supposed to keep up with you when you don't want to be kept up with?"

I don't have an answer for this. Maybe I'm just the bad guy.

When I don't say anything, Mom looks at the floor.

She doesn't try to stop me from leaving. I weave my way through tables of happy families, teenagers giggling and drinking milk tea boba, and an ancient couple talking in Swedish by a window. When I look behind me, my mother hasn't moved. I leave Penny Mainquist in Yndo, a statue, forever.

On the way out, I hold the door open for a younger girl with ginger hair and a backward cap. She blinks at me with wide eyes.

"No way," she says. "You're —" Her hand flies to her mouth. "Oh my God! How are you since the band broke up? Is everything good? Do you think I could get a picture with you?"

"I'm sorry. I'm late for a meeting." I only wish I had a meeting to be late to. I move past her, but then glance back, swimming with guilt. "Everything is fine. Thank you for asking."

When I get back to my car, the thermostat tells me it is seventy degrees out. Cold and getting colder as the sun goes down. The tips of the trees turn into molten gold.

• • • •

Luckily for me, by the time I finish speeding to the Temptation, Annabel hasn't even gone on yet. I shoulder my way through the crowd and find Ocelle and Lily in the heat. They shout at me that they're happy to see me, giddy with the smoky air.

"How was dinner with your mom?" Lily yells at me.

"Shit," I yell back. "Left after five minutes."

"Yeesh." She comes closer and leans against me. She's cute tonight, looking seventies — a handkerchief in her hair and everything. She smells like an odd mix of tequila and wildflowers. "Well, we're glad you're here and not there."

"For *cer*tain," Ocelle says. He winks at me without smiling.

Annabel's set is fantastic. She starts with a couple of old favorites, but then she hits the audience with a few even I and Ocelle have never heard. She's fantastic. She may have her stern beliefs about not being a solo act, but damn, she could do it if she wanted to. The place is dim and crowded, and I've long been disaccustomed to what it's like in an audience, but I find my face fighting off smiles more and more. Lily makes me dance with her, and I see Ocelle whirling around and hopping like he couldn't be happier if I asked him to. It's refreshing. For the first time since before the band broke up, I figure maybe things can turn out alright at some point.

There's a moment where I think I see Piper in the crowd. There she is, all lace and silk and satin and pearls. A hummingbird drenched in her fine, exquisite fabrics. My entire body freezes, and I become a statue, bewitched by her again, as cursed as it is. I remembered finding her, her feet intertwining with her drummer's in the sheets, the sound of lust echoing down the hallway. I'd been meaning to surprise her. It was her birthday. I had flowers.

I look down at Lily, who pulls me away from the place, bless her, and I try to forget as soon as I step through the doors.

FIFTEEN

I unlocked the front door and stepped inside, the bouquet digging into the creases of my palm. A birthday surprise for Piper. I was so excited.

Her apartment was small, tinier than mine, but cute: white lace, antiques from the local Goodwill, a miniature bed for her toy poodle Stella. The lights were off, the living room unoccupied and almost arctic in its nature.

That's when the sounds started to filter in. I don't remember when exactly I'd become aware of them, only that they were suddenly happening, and whatever they were, I didn't like them.

Quickly I deposited the bouquet on Piper's kitchen counter and made my way down the hall, passing framed photos of kittens and roses. The bedroom door was ajar, and behind it, the sounds were louder: gasps and whimpers, giggles and sighs.

Feet. Socked feet, intertwining, rumpled beneath pink silk covers.

"Micah," Piper giggled. "Micah, *stop,* we're going to get in trouble."

Micah. *Her drummer's name,* I thought. My stomach began to churn and, swearing at myself, I stepped through the threshold.

Piper caught my eye first, and yelped when she saw me, disconnecting from Micah and pulling the covers up over her bare chest. Micah looked up, too, and saw me — "what the hell, man?" — and that was that. Any part of me that I thought could have healed broke again.

For a moment I just looked at Piper. Disregarding Micah. The art on the walls. The smell of skin.

I scratched the back of my neck. "I left you some flowers," I said. "On the — on the counter. For when you're... finished."

Piper didn't say anything. She studied me, and I swear her eyes were brimming with tears.

I turned and left.

SIXTEEN

After Annabel is done, we don't stick around to watch the high school kid. We parade our little solo ukulele artist out into the street and celebrate her.

"Man, that was so good," Lily says, messing with Annabel's fingers, Ocelle's big jacket draped over her shoulders. It is getting cold fast; I shiver with jealousy. "You're so *good*, Annabel."

"Well, thanks."

"I mean it," Lily says, and we echo this. "Are you ready to go to Jude's?"

"Jude's?" I repeat. I stop walking, and the others turn to face me. Jude is Lily's older brother, who'd graduated a couple of years before us; he was our go-to guy for any drinks or pot. I hadn't heard from him in a long time. "We're going to Jude's?"

Lily nods. "He's having a party tonight," she says. "At his house. And we figured if we weren't going to stay to watch that high school kid, we could all go and see if it's any fun."

"Oh. Am I allowed to tag along?"

Ocelle rolls his eyes. In the more natural light, he looks a little worse for wear, the bottom of his lacy dress in tatters, the tips of his combat boots scuffed and graying. "*No*, Stars, you can't come," he scoffs. "That's why Lily mentioned it, just to brag. You're not invited."

"Funny."

I drove here, so I tell them I'll meet them there. Ten minutes later, I'm turning onto the street that leads to Jude's neighborhood: a beautiful red brick city with trees lining the avenue, the type of big, grand oaks you'd see in a movie scene. I park on the curb of a nearby rich neighbor — ballsy — and step out. It's gotten fully dark now. I'm not dressed for a party at all, I'm sure I'll look like an idiot in there, but I'm too depleted of energy to care.

Lily, Annabel, and Ocelle arrive soon too. They're all gorgeous. They look like Italian sketches — what is that word? *Abbozzos.* They look like abbozzos, in beautiful thrift store clothing and homemade makeup looks and tiny tattoos. Next to them, I look like a ghost.

Lily bounds up to me in the driveway when she sees me, a big kid-like smile on her face. "Are you *so* excited?" she asks.

"Uh-huh."

She grabs me by the hand and pulls me up the walk, Annabel and Ocelle not far behind. Behind the front door, noise erupts. Yes, this is definitely Jude's house. Lily knocks, and soon he appears, clearly already baked.

"Hey, finally," he says, as Lily hugs him. He looks past her and sees me. "Oh, hey, Stars. How've you been?"

"Fine, you?"

He grins. "Well, it could be worse, y'know? C'mon in."

The house is big and ugly and stuffed with people. If it weren't for my friends, I wouldn't know a single soul here. The familiar smells hang in the air: weed, sweat, a hint of vomit somewhere or other. The music is atrociously loud. I'd hoped we could all move together as a pack, but the moment I turn around, I'm alone. No one I know in sight, not even Jude.

This will be a long night. I make my way through the crowd and eventually find the kitchen, where most of the punch is already gone; I use the ladle and scoop some of the dregs of it anyway. It tastes sour as hell. It reminds me of one of the cocktails at the first ever bar we played, years and years ago. Girls are giggling and dancing together, a few guys are playing beer pong over in the dining room with Jude at the helm. Ah. There he is.

I'm not the biggest fan of parties.

After drinking a little more, I move through a hallway of people all cramped shoulder-to-shoulder. I feel a hand brush against my neck and turn to see a beautiful girl. She looks me up and down and then smiles at me, arching well-kept eyebrows.

"Well, well," she says over the music. "I didn't know Mothic Wreckage was playing here tonight."

"Who?"

Her name, as I will come to discover, is Sophi. She makes a point of telling me it doesn't have an E. I like it, I tell her; it falls off the tongue, eager to escape and be heard. This makes her laugh at me. Before I know it, we're upstairs, in what I suppose is Jude's room. His unmade bed. It's the quietest place we could find.

Sophi is kind to me. She and I have fun. She reminds me of all the tour girls, of Greta and Georgia and Alice, but she's better somehow. Her long black hair makes me just about go insane, it's so pretty. Her eyeliner is sharp, wild, bright gold against her skin. Together, we sit on Jude's bed, our hands intertwining, and when we are finally finished, she pulls away to breathe and grins at me. Downstairs, the music continues to play.

"That was nice," she says.

"Yeah."

"But you look worried."

"What?"

Her head tilts. "I said you look worried about something," she repeats. "Is everything okay?" Her expression morphs into one of extreme alarm. "Oh, God. You have a girlfriend, don't you? That Piper girl from that Aphrodite band or whatever?"

"No, no, no," I hurry, holding out my hands to placate her. "No, it's not that. I just... I don't know. I'm not a big party guy. I don't know if I'm doing it right."

Sophi laughs goodnaturedly. "But you're the Mothic Wreckage guy."

"Well, I was. But even then, it wasn't exactly like I was the one doing much of the partying."

Sophi looks down and grabs her bag from the carpeted floor of the room. Her hands are nice. I study them while I wait for her gaze to find me again. Her fingers are long, thin, and spindly, but charming. They glint with rings. She starts to take stuff out of her bag: tangled earphones, an anime keycard, and a little enamel pin of a glass of lemonade. When Sophi sits back up, she's holding a small tab of blotting paper with a single red heart in the center. "If you're stressed, then try this," she suggests kindly. "It'll help, I swear. I used to swear by this stuff in college."

I take the paper in my palm and ponder it. "What is it?"

"It's acid, but like, the *good* kind. You'll see the universe for what it is and whatever else. Trust me, you'll like it."

I should not be this much of an idiot, but I am starting to feel stressed. The dinner I had with my mother earlier still grates on my mind. So does being here alone, on my own. And even worse, for some terrible reason, I can't stop thinking about Monday night, when Ocelle had leaned into my face as if to kiss it.

Ocelle, you're not thinking clearly.

I never do. That's what makes me so cool.

I stick the tab under my tongue. Sophi smiles at me warmly. "Cool," she says. "Might kick in after a few minutes. Just be patient. Hey, you want me to go get you some water?"

"Oh, would you?"

"Sure." She stands and grabs her bag. "Back soon."

She vanishes behind the door and out into the hallway. For a few minutes, I scroll on my phone, and before long, I forget that I've taken anything. Maybe I feel a little groggier, but oh well.

I hear a noise. I think it is Sophi coming back with my water, when I look up, Cal is standing in the room.

For a moment, all we do is stare at each other. He's a sight for sore eyes. He looks so normal, so well. But so unhappy.

"You're such an idiot," Cal says, folding his arms. "What, you're left alone for, like, ten minutes and then you start taking random drugs from girls you don't know?"

I start to panic. "What do I do, then?" He doesn't answer. "Cal, what do I *do*?"

"Why would I know?"

I've never tried acid before. I curse myself. I should have done it at home, safely, in the comforting presence of Ocelle and Lily and whoever else. The room is colorful now. A little louder. The humming air conditioner makes me want to cut my ears off. There are things on the walls I don't remember being there before.

Moths. There are moths on the walls.

I press my hands against the bed's messed-up comforter as if that will anchor me where I am. "Cal, I'm scared," I admit, studying the pattern of the blanket.

"I mean, that's kind of on you. You know you used to swear against this stuff." In the corner of my eye, I see him sit on the floor. "You're different now, Stars. Sleeping with all those girls on tour —"

"You know about that?"

"— and all that pot, I mean, *come on*."

"I'm sorry." My eyes start to blur with tears. "I don't want you to be mad at me, that was never my intention."

"And then you threw the band away altogether?" Cal asks, rolling his eyes. "I mean, Jesus. Why did I even ask you to start it in the first place? Why am I here? Why do you associate me with every little fucking thing?"

I shut my eyes tight and put my hands over my ears. I know this isn't real, but it feels like it is. I feel like Cal's standing right over me, his face contorting and melting, and he is so incredibly angry with me. I can't bring myself to open my eyes and look to see if I'm right. My heart begins to pound, my forehead begins to sweat.

I yelp when I feel someone's hand close around my wrist. I open my eyes to see Ocelle.

"Hey," he says, holding up his other hand. "There you are. I finally found you. What are you doing in here?"

I look past him. Cal is gone. The moths have multiplied, joined by spiders and cockroaches and ladybugs. The entire room has become an insect paradise.

"I — I —" I can hardly get words out, I'm so scared. My throat has closed with fear. "Some girl gave me a tab to take, she said it'd be fun, it was acid, I've never had acid before, fuck, I don't know, I'm freaking out, there are bugs all over the walls, holy shit —"

"Hey," Ocelle says again, gentler this time. He cups my cheek in his hand, and I grab his fingers, grateful for the warmth, for the touch of something real. He smirks like I said something funny. "In the future, let's refrain from taking drugs from random people we don't know, hmm? Come on. Let's get you out of here."

• • • •

It takes a long time, but eventually, Ocelle manages to get me downstairs. I am surprised by how much time has passed. The clock tells me it is past two, but I have quickly learned not to trust anything I see. I cling to Ocelle like he's my lifeline as we maneuver through the crowd. I see birds. Bugs. Strange shapes. Books on library shelves. Visual snow. A couple of times, I see something that stops me dead in my tracks: Cal's body sprawled on the couch, contorted with pain, or everyone in the room peppered with shattered glass. If it weren't for Ocelle, I'd fall on the floor and cry.

The next thing I am cognizant of is standing outside Jude's house on the driveway, leaning against Ocelle, who is warm and smells good. Lily and Annabel are there, too, but I'm not paying attention to them. The night air is brisk and cool, offensively so.

"I don't know what the fuck he was thinking," I hear Ocelle grumble, "but I'm gonna get him home. I have a feeling it's going to be a long night."

Out in the middle of the street, the asphalt melts and cracks until it is not a street but a craggy abyss.

"Hey, Stars?" Ocelle asks, his voice light and sweet. He turns me towards him and shakes me gently. "Hey. Where'd you park?"

"Aren't you drunk or something?" I manage. I think I might be yelling. "You can't drive."

"I'm fine. I'd pass a breathalyzer. Where'd you park?"

I think we say goodbye to Annabel and Lily soon after that. Then we are in the car. It's so hot. I have the air conditioner blowing, but the air against my skin feels like ant bites. Ocelle is driving, his eyes glued to the road, but occasionally I hear him amidst the chaos: "You're okay. Hang in there. We're almost home." I can't tell but I think I might be sobbing.

Thankfully we make it back home alright. Ocelle helps me inside. The apartment is a sight for sore eyes, completely and utterly bug-free. There are a couple of people in the living room — my mother, my sisters, writing letters of apology to me — but other than that, it's home sweet home.

Ocelle leads me back into the bedroom (pausing in the kitchen to grab a bottle of water) and sits me down. Dimly, I'm aware of how similar this is to that other more heinous night, which is why I ended up taking that damn tab in the first place. I sit on Cal's half of the bed.

"It was acid, for sure," Ocelle says, studying my face.

"I'm going crazy. I'm losing my mind."

"No, you're not." His calmness is shocking to me. He reaches over and grabs a bottle of water. "Just hold my hand. You'll come down from outer space sooner or later."

"I'm gonna die. I'm *going* to die."

"You're not going to die. You took acid, that's all. Drink your water."

That's how most of the night goes. I sit up, ramrod straight, on Cal's half of our bed, holding Ocelle's hand and drinking water and eating food when I can tolerate it, and occasionally I'll point at something and go "WHAT IS *THAT?*" and Ocelle will have to explain to me that that's the dresser, that's a mirror, that's a sticky note. Not my father, glowering. Not Cal's face, studying me with disappointment, his chest a gaping hole. At one point I ask Ocelle to hold onto me because I feel like my skin will start falling off if he doesn't keep me together. I stare at the ceiling, eyes snapped wide open, dimly aware that I'm in his arms. I can feel his chin on the top of my head.

There's a moth on the ceiling. "Ocelle," I say, panic creeping back in.

"You're okay. I've got you."

There are so many things I want to say to him. I would if I could figure out how my mouth works. I want to say *I love you, I want to say I hate you, why did you break up the band, we were so happy.* A million different things.

Finally, I find words. "I saw Cal," I say, my voice a harsh whisper. I can barely hear myself talking. Tears well up and fall. I can't take my eyes off the ceiling. "I saw him. He was so upset with me."

Ocelle kisses the top of my head and holds me closer. I feel his hand on my cheek. "Cal wasn't upset with you. I promise."

"He was. He said *why do you keep fucking all those girls on tour, why do you do drugs...*"

"Cal wasn't mad at you, Stars."

It is the softest, sweetest, gentlest thing Ocelle has ever said to me.

I stay in Ocelle's arms for many more hours, until I finally start to come out of the trip. I keep talking, saying bleary nonsense about Cal and my parents and how much I miss the band, and Ocelle listens.

He holds me close and he listens.

SEVENTEEN

The next morning, I walk back into Conan's about thirty minutes late and find Ramiro waiting for me, eyebrows arched, foot a-tapping.

"Look who decided to join us," he says dramatically, scratching his cheek with his middle finger. "I so kindly let you off early last night, and then you repay me by being a half hour behind schedule? Come on, man. Hop to it."

I nod and head back toward the break room. It's difficult not to turn around and tell him it's not such a big deal since there aren't any customers in here anyway, but he has already gone back to dusting the ultimate Jimi Hendrix collection sitting in the window, on sale for $64.99.

Ocelle was happy to take care of me. We had fallen asleep last night, and he was still out like a light when I'd awoken. I left him a note thanking him for seeing me through to the end of my trip and told him I'd be back after work.

I think about last night as I'm sorting the A-J aisle of CDs. Cal. Ocelle. The whole thing had had a profoundly odd tenderness to it, leaving a hollow sweet taste in my mouth, as if I'd long ago had a piece of candy but nothing to wash it down with.

"Hey, Juniper," Ramiro says as the door opens and shuts again. He is now sweeping the floor.

Juniper is the only other employee. I think I have mentioned her before. She is a junior at the local high school, and she cares about this job even less than I do. She nods her good morning to us and turns on the radio we have next to the cash register. She likes to listen to the dating segment, told by Gella Anderson and Roshni Kumari: "Gella and Roshni's 'Does She Like Mes?'" Every morning at ten sharp.

I glance at the clock. It's fifteen-till. When the radio buzzes on, I hear the usual daytime announcer, Daira, talking about me. Well, not entirely about me.

"— since Mothic Wreckage's tragic separation a few months ago," she was saying. "Well, we're happy to report former member Kento Kim — y'know, the drummer — he's got a solo EP coming out next month: 'I Hope I'm Crazy.'"

Ramiro and Juniper look over at me. I glance up at the sound of Kento's name, shocked. Kento, releasing a solo EP? I'd texted him a few times over the past couple of weeks, but otherwise seen or heard nothing of him.

"I can't spoil too much," Daira is saying, "but rest assured, Kento's talent doesn't stop at *just* the drums. He's got some singing chops like you wouldn't believe. I wish we'd gotten to see him take that role in Mothic Wreckage sometimes. Not that Stars Mainquist wasn't great, but, y'know..."

Juniper reaches over and pushes the antenna back into its slot.

"Did you know about that?" Ramiro asks, leaning against the broom.

I shake my head. "Hadn't heard a single word."

"Hmm. Maybe he wanted it to be a surprise."

Or maybe he didn't want us to know because Ocelle would raise a huge fuss. Both are reasonable options.

I keep working. In no time at all, my phone is buzzing, and I head into the break room to answer it. Of course, it's Ocelle.

I put the phone to my ear. "Hello."

"'*I HOPE I'M CRAZY?*' What the fuck? What the *fuck*?!"

"Calm down. I'm sure it has nothing to do with us."

"Yes, the fuck it does!" Ocelle says. "It has everything to do with us. We've been with Kento since the beginning. He could have at least given us the courtesy of announcing an EP to us before the rest of the world. Weren't you trying to get Mothic Wreckage back on its feet? He's just gonna jeopardize all that?"

"Calm down," I say again, but he's right. This is an impairment to my plans. My strategy had been to help Ocelle get better again, and then talk to Annabel and Kento about maybe reassembling, maybe working on the album. They both knew that was the plan, too; I'd told them, after all.

Annabel's little in-town gigs were a tad annoying, but forgivable. Kento going behind everyone's backs and releasing an entire EP by himself was not a good start.

"I'm *so* pissed," Ocelle grumbles. "I might text him."

"Don't," I say.

"Well, what am I supposed to do?"

"Just try and relax. Do a face mask. Do some yoga. It'll be okay, we'll talk about it."

"Whatever. I'll figure it out."

He hangs up the phone. I stare at the screen, dumbfounded.

I spend the rest of the day cleaning the store in a daze, ringing up albums for people at the front counter and saying, "No, I'm sorry, I haven't heard of that band. Mothic *What*age?" A couple of people don't fall for it.

When I come home, Ocelle is smoking. I step through the doorway and a cloud of weed smell hits me in the face.

"Ocelle," I say, heading around the corner and depositing my bag on the floor. He's not in the living room; he has the door out to the patio open, smoking as he watches the sunset behind the neighbors' trees. He holds his joint carefully, bringing it to his lips like it's a chalice in a sacrifice. He hasn't heard me yet.

I step out onto the patio and he doesn't look at me. He only leans back in his chair, curling one of his locks around a bored finger. He is sketching hands and flowers on a yellowed notepad. His eyes look blue in the evening light.

"Well," he finally says, "at least he's doing what makes him happy."

I hold out my hand and Ocelle gives me the joint. I take a hit from it; it's some strong stuff. I hand it back without much complaint.

"I don't know, Stars," Ocelle says bitterly. "Maybe it was me. Maybe it was my fault."

"What was?"

He waves his hand vaguely. He's wearing a sweater and torn corduroy pants, fishnets peeking out from the holes. "The band. All of it."

"It wasn't anyone's fault. Sometimes shit just doesn't work."

He looks at me and laughs like I'm crazy. "Are you kidding?" he asks. "You do realize you should be on a stage somewhere right now, performing to an audience of people who are in love with you? You should have people offering to shine your shoes every time you step out of the tour van. And *I* should be somewhere glamorous, flashing my cigarettes around like a rich lady. Fucking Marilyn Monroe. But here we are. I'm a loiterer and you're working at the record store. Isn't that just *la vie en rose?*"

I hate to admit it but he's right. Life was supposed to be so much more than this.

There's still Annabel's gigs. She has a couple more towards the end of the month. At the first, she flounders, clearly unsure of herself as she strums on the ukulele. The second one is more sure-footed, more reminiscent of her old Mothic Wreckage playing. She barks her lyrics into the microphone and the ground shakes with the power of her words. I've said it a million times but if she wants the success for herself, she could have it. There's no debating it.

After the gig, we're all hanging out backstage when a stagehand materializes next to me, putting a hand on my shoulder. "Hey," he says quietly. "I'm really sorry to bother you, but a girl's asking if she can see you."

I look up at him, confused. "This isn't a Mothic Wreckage concert."

"I know, I know," the stagehand quickly corrects. "But she — she saw you come back here, I guess. She says she's your sister."

Annabel and I look at each other. Ocelle bursts out laughing and Lily swats him on the arm.

"Okay," I say to the stagehand, standing. "Thanks for letting me know."

· · · ·

I meet her behind the venue.

She looks a lot younger than she really is, in a green halter top and the tiniest blue jean shorts I've ever seen. Nothing like the conservative sister I grew up alongside — because it's definitely still her, the same plain face. We have the same eyes, the same hands, the same voice.

It's Violet.

"Hi," she says when she sees me. She blinks. Her eyes are a startling blue, peeking out behind glasses that are a lot like my own. "I'm really happy to see you, Stars."

At least she gives me the quiet dignity of my preferred name.

"What can I do for you?" I ask.

She shrugs. "I don't want anything. I just miss you. I had to see you. I thought it would be easy to catch you after one of Annabel's shows."

"Smart sleuthing," I say.

I can't read her expression. She rubs her bare arms, shivers as the wind blows. When my parents found out about me and Cal, they weren't happy; I'd loved my sisters and expected them to be on my side, but they'd turned against me too. It had broken my heart. I had essentially been kicked out of the house. Neither Violet nor Rosa ever lent a helping hand to me, and I just can't forgive it. I remember, so vividly, being a freshman in high school and sitting sandwiched between my two sisters in the pews of the Blanchet City Church. Mr. Brown was doing the sermon, all about the perfect marriage — my parents sat attentively, listening to all that rabble about women in white. It was a good sermon — Mr. Brown had a great, big, booming voice, pleasing to listen to — but I squirmed uncomfortably at the content of his words, picturing with unhappiness the cute boy from my English class. A boy who, I would come to learn, was named Calvin Roberts.

"How are you?" Violet asks. "Genuinely. Since the band, since Piper, since..." Her voice falters. I know what she's going to say. *Since Cal.* The funeral that none of them showed up to.

"I'm fine." My voice comes out more clipped than I mean it to, and I think it hurts her, because she blinks a little, startled. "I'm doing fine. I'm happy."

"We're all worried about you," she says.

"I'm fine," I repeat, a little louder this time.

"Fuck." Violet runs a hand through her dark brown hair. When she looks at me again, it is with a fixed glare. "Stars, look. I'm sorry. Alright? I came to say that I'm sorry for everything that happened. I know you loved Cal, and I should have had the balls to side with you about it. I should have defended you against everyone else. It's haunted me. It still does. It always will. But I just couldn't go another day without telling you how I felt."

I study her. We used to be close when we were little. Now there's a gaping chasm between us. Her words come across that void to me, but awkwardly, as if they're in another language that neither of us really speak. "Why now?" I ask. I can barely hear myself over the rush of blood in my head. I've been imagining this conversation for years. "Why here?"

"Because I'm gonna kill myself if I have to wait any longer," Violet says, wringing her hands. "After the band fell apart, I knew I had to make things right. I miss you. I miss you so much. And I'm not here on behalf of Mom, or Rosa, or anyone — just me. I just want us to be okay again. I understand if it can't happen, but..."

Without really thinking, I pull her into a hug.

For a minute she doesn't know what to do. And then she deflates, leaning her head against my shoulder. Her hair billows, a familiar smell. A smell I've grown up with.

"I never stopped loving you," I admit, despite myself. "I never could. I was just angry."

"And you had every right to be," Violet supplies, rubbing my back with her hand. "I want to move forward. I want to be there for you."

I sigh in relief, too. For a long time I held onto anger, a special reserve of anger, just for my family — and now I let go of some of it for Violet, and it feels good. Better than I thought it would feel. I hug her tightly, and for the first time in years, I feel like I'm home.

Things are better after that.

EIGHTEEN

More and more days pass. I keep in touch with Kento, but all we talk about is the EP. Not the band, not Ocelle, not the future in any respect. There's an unspoken rule. I know Kento isn't asking after Ocelle because he's angry and because Ocelle's still angry. I like to pretend my bandmates are men but really, most days they are just children fighting over toys. Annabel agrees with me on this.

Speaking of Annabel, she and Lily begin dating pretty soon after Kento's EP is announced. They're nice together: all clumsy hands in the dark and matching lockets and dried roses and dates at bakeries. I can't pretend I'm not happy for them. Lily is an old friend of mine and she's been looking for this happiness since before we met. But seeing two hands intertwining, watching a pair of lips kiss a freckled cheek — these things send me to a bad place.

Lily loved Cal so much. The three of us, along with Cal's sister Camilla, were sort of like the four musketeers of our high school. Practically inseparable. Lily and Cal, in particular, had always been close. They loved to sing together. That's actually how I got into playing the guitar; they'd needed an accompanist, as neither of them knew how to play.

Lily was arm-in-arm with me on the day of the funeral. She didn't leave for a second. While we were getting ready, she brushed my hair, fixed my tie, smoothed my lapel. She did everything just right. I'd cursed that morning, shaming it for having the balls to be so sunny and pretty. She'd listened and scorned it right along with me.

She'd been there on that final night, too. In the waiting room. I'd been unable to cry for a few hours, but as soon as I saw her come through the doors — the LED clock on the wall reading three in the morning — I broke into sobs.

I'd said to her, my cold, shaky hands in hers, "I don't know what to do, Lily. I don't fucking know."

"Tell me what to do," had been her answer, "and I will go do it."

So I said, could you please go back home and grab some of the Watermelon Daytime out of the fridge, could you turn the bathroom light off and shut the door behind you and maybe also grab me a sweater or something, it's quite cold in here.

She did it all. She kissed all my tears and held me until someone, somewhere in that godforsaken building, could finally give me a clear answer. A timeline. A verdict.

She wasn't in the room when Cal went, but she did get to say goodbye, if only briefly. I think about that often: the way she touched him, lovingly, like Camilla might have. The way she kissed him on the temple and held his hand and said, "Handsome boy. I love you."

The anniversary of Cal's death is August the fifteenth. I do not do anything on August fifteenth. I curl up in Cal's half of the bed and think about him, trying to remember how he smelled, how it felt to hold his hand. Four years is a long time to be without someone you loved so completely, so wholly and unapologetically. Sometimes I shame myself for the mere fact I could ever forget any piece of him, from the way his eyes crinkled when he smiled to the way he told a joke to the way he danced around this room like no one was watching, the music blaring.

This August fifteenth, I take off work. I wake from an uneasy sleep on the couch and trudge into the bedroom, where Ocelle is still out like a light. Trying not to wake him, I slide into the bed too. The feeling of two bodies in one bed is so familiar that I catch my breath.

For a while I do nothing but look through photos I have of Cal on my phone. I took a lot, and I'm really glad I did. There's one of him sitting right where I am, looking out the window, the sunlight peeking in through the blinds. One of us laughing with friends: Lily, Camilla, and the two of us, all holding cotton candy sticks. One of him I took in the park; we'd met a dog and he'd played fetch with it. And my favorite photo of all, the one we took in Mexico: the two of us in front of a pier in Quintana Roo, my lips pressed against his cheek, Cal mid-laugh. His freckled face, frozen forever.

My hand hovers over that photo for a minute. I don't remember what he'd been laughing at. I wish to God I knew now. That trip was one we took just after he'd been diagnosed. We debated whether or not we should even go, but Cal insisted; he wanted to see the ocean one last time.

He curled up against me and breathed in deeply, the sea wind whipping through his hair. Underneath us, the blanket shifted. The waves lapped against the shore.

I held him close. Even here, in such a peaceful place, he was trembling from exhaustion, his hands gripping mine firmly. I brushed locks of hair out of his face and kissed him on the temple. Laughing slightly, he reached up and returned the favor by brushing his lips against the underside of my jaw.

I pointed out at the water, running my thumb over his knuckles with my other hand. "See all that?" I asked him softly. "That's all the love I have for you. All that water."

"Corny."

"It's true." I kissed him again, all over this time. "I love you so much."

"I love you too," he said quietly. A pause, and then: "I'm gonna miss the beach."

"I know."

Two broken hearts on the shore.

I miss him so much. His hidden birthmarks. His honey lips. The way he'd press flowers into his brown hair, the way he could never handle spicy food but ate it anyway. He loved movie dates. He loved stealing my earbuds. He was sunshine.

Next to me, Ocelle shifts, and I instinctively shut my phone off. "What are you doing here?" he mumbles haughtily as if he owns the place. He rubs his eyes and sits up, giving me a tired smile. "How rude must you be?"

"I live here," I tell him.

"Mm. I forgot. What day is it?"

"The fifteenth."

"Oh." Ocelle yawns and returns his head to the pillow, turning over. He fidgets with the strawberry candle on his side of the bed, making a grab for the butane lighter and not quite making it. "So that means you'll be moping around all day and you won't let anyone talk to you about it. That's today, isn't it?"

"Yeah, that's today." Lily has just sent me a text: *four years later and it hasn't gotten any easier. i love you.*

"Well, good," Ocelle says. "I hope you have fun."

"Thanks."

It would not be fun.

I think Ocelle is going to leave it at that, but he sits back up again and looks at me. His hair is so messy. "Mmm, no," he decides, "that won't do. Tell you what. Tonight we'll go out to a big fancy dinner, the two of us, and we'll sit and talk and laugh and pretend we care about things that we don't."

"No, thanks. I'd just rather be alone with my thoughts today."

I start to open my phone again, but Ocelle's hand reaches over and turns it off. "No," he says. "You ought to go on an adventure with me. We're going out to dinner. Have fun sulking until then, but at seven, we're going out. No complaining."

I don't put up much of a fight. Lily comes over a little after noon, bearing cheek kisses and a stuffed bear. I watch cartoons and take a long walk, looking for squirrels and deer on the path.

Then, at seven in the evening, there I am — standing in front of Lachere's in a button-down and slacks. I look sharper than I thought I would. Ocelle looks great. He has on a frilly chiffon shirt, the type of thing you can see at any nightclub, but somehow he makes it elegant —

that and high-waisted jeans, clean and simple and not fancy enough for this restaurant.

He turns to smile at me proudly, the gloss on his lips catching in the light. "Well, I've picked a good spot," he says. "*Après toi, monsieur.*"

The inside is hushed and warm. Our table is in a golden corner of the big room, between two quartz pillars. Dimly I wonder where Ocelle thinks we've gotten the money for this stashed. The waiter, a snotty-looking British man with olive green eyes, seats us and takes our orders — water for me, and an incredibly expensive bottle of champagne for Ocelle. After the man has gone, Ocelle nods like it is nothing special.

"Just a little treat," he says, watching the candle on the table flickering, "for what I can only assume is a sad day in the life of Stars Mainquist."

"Ha. Yeah."

"You've never told me much about it," he says hesitantly.

"I know. It's... personal."

Ocelle arches an eyebrow and laughs. "Personal," he repeats. "Listen, you know as well as *any*one that I won't pry, but if you want to talk to me, you know you can trust me, right?"

"It's not fair if you want me to spill my guts without you also offering something."

I look at my hands, webbed and veiny in the dim restaurant light. I can't wait until the waiter comes back with some bread and oil; my stomach grumbles. I haven't eaten all day, as is my August fifteenth tradition.

"Fine. I'll go first." Ocelle flips some hair over his shoulder. "My name's not Ocelle." I look at him. He smiles victoriously. "What, you thought my parents gave me a name like that?" he asks with a giggle. "You're funny. No. No, Ocelle is an identity I chose for myself."

I stare at him.

"Do you remember," he says, "what I told you about my name the day we met? You remember what Ocelle *means*, don't you?"

"It — it's a term of endearment," I stammer. "In Latin."

"Precisely." His golden eyeshadow, done to complement the theme of the room, is driving me insane. "Sort of like calling someone your darling. The apple of your eye."

"Right."

He shakes his head, flowery curls bobbing as he does so. "Growing up, I was no one's darling," he says softly. "I was the apple of no one's eye. Not even my parents. Well, they liked me, sure, but they had other priorities, which is fine. I understand that. But, oh, how I longed to be *loved*." His smile has disappeared for a moment, but here it returns, back and brighter than ever. "And so as soon as I turned eighteen, I decided for myself," he says contentedly. "I became *Ocelle* Galler — so every time anyone, anyone speaks to me, it will be with love. It will be with *adoration*." He spreads his hands widely and grins like he couldn't be more pleased with himself. "It worked," he says, softer now. "Everyone loves me all the time, and I *deserve* it."

For a moment I don't say anything.

"Well?" Ocelle prompts.

"Well, what?"

"What do you think of that?"

"I think you're insane," I say, and to my surprise, he leans his head back and laughs serenely.

"Maybe," he concedes. "But that's just one of my many faces."

The waiter brings the bread and oil. It is not as good as homemade bread, the kind Cal used to make. But the waiter keeps our glasses filled, mine with water and Ocelle's with various fizzing drinks. Our conversation fumbles along steadily until he comes and disappears until he leaves again, the back of his black vest meshing into the billions of others around the room.

"Your turn," Ocelle purrs. The waiter has just left, but already his glass is empty again, a thin line of champagne twinkling at the bottom. "Tell me something. Here, I know: what is it about August the fifteenth again? I keep forgetting. Is it the anniversary of your being cast down from heaven or something?"

I shake my head and stare at the white tablecloth, flawless except for a few spattered drops of water, well on their way to drying. The oil has been mostly sopped up, the bread now a thin crust on a plate. Around us, people chatter and laugh, families and business associates and lovers. I am with Ocelle. I was a musician, once, and I am with someone I played music with.

"I," I start. My voice is as soft as it ever has been, just a hoarse whisper, so quiet that I sense Ocelle leaning forward to hear me better. "I lost him."

I look at Ocelle furtively, expecting some snide reply, but there is none. He studies me intently, waiting for me to say more.

"I lost him today," I say. I can't think of much else, only those last sad few hours.

"It's Cal's day, right?" Ocelle asks. His voice has donned some new, familiar understanding.

My instinct is to shrink away from him. I get the sense he's going to keep interrogating me: asking for names, details, and autopsies. Instead, he leans back in his chair and straightens out the cuffs of his yellow shirt.

"Well, I'm sorry for your loss. I must have said that about a thousand times," Ocelle says in a sweet, plain voice. "I hope I haven't made today more difficult for you."

"No." I put my chin in the palm of my hand. "It was easier this time around. At least I ate."

Ocelle nods. He's seen me on three other August fifteenths exactly like this one, filled with me trudging around my apartment in old sweatpants and greasy, un-showered hair and red, near-feverish cheeks.

He and Annabel and Kento know today well. It was a Sabbath: I would not rehearse with the band, I would not even think about touching my guitar, and I would not do one nice thing for myself. I would look through photos and pity myself until it was August sixteenth, and then I would get back to work.

Ocelle raises his empty glass as solemnly as if he were drinking to his demise. "To you, then, the very essence of an Orpheus," he says, "on your sad, sad day."

If I were an idiot, this would be when I lean over the table, disregarding the bread crust, disregarding the oil dish, to kiss him. Today I long to be touched, to be wanted, to be perceived and accepted. That will do. Stars will do.

Instead, I only let the rim of my glass kiss his, and the dinner continues in silence, the two of us only people who've made music together once more.

· · · ·

C al had decided, quite close to the end, that he wanted an art exhibit.

I knew it was a bad idea. I tried to warn him. He was overexerting himself, not resting the way he should have been, hobbling to and fro across the museum floor when he should have been in bed with me. But I couldn't deter him. The exhibit itself was beautiful. Photos and artworks about his time as a terminally ill young man. Sculptures made of oxygen tubing and pill boxes. It was a gorgeous assortment, and as I stood next to him, watching the people mill around, I could feel his excitement.

"They like it, Stars," he said softly. "I mean, they really, *really* like it."

"Of course they do." My arm found its familiar place around his waist. "It's yours."

Lily was there, of course, celebrating him. She bounded from piece to piece, all smiles, taking photos on her silly disposable camera. When she reached us, she said, "Smile!" and pointed it at the two of us before we had any chance to react.

That's the last photo I have of Cal. At that point it was a matter of hours.

After a quick dinner with Lily (Cal's favorite: Korean fried chicken), we went home. We touched. We kissed. We said goodbye. And sometime in the night, Cal had gotten up, and I heard him from down the hall, calling my name in a soft little animalistic bray.

He died the next morning.

I told him the exhibit was a bad idea.

NINETEEN

Taylor's is a sight for sore eyes.

I head in there on one of my days off. Annabel has wanted to meet for drinks, and she said what better place for that than where it all began? I head inside a little after noon, my jacket damp from the sprinkling clouds outside. I miss the feeling of sunlight hitting my skin. It has rained for weeks.

Annabel is already at the bar, a ball of nervous energy, though it looks like she hasn't ordered anything. I slide onto the stool next to her. Rigby is nowhere to be seen.

"Hey," Annabel says without looking at me. Her soft hair, so dark brown it's almost black, is frizzy from mistreatment. She traces over a couple of cocktail names on the menu with a finger. "How are you?"

"I'm fine. How are you?"

"Fine." Silence. "How was your little acid trip?"

"Oh," I say, startled. I'd forgotten all about it. "Ocelle got me through it. I'm okay now."

Annabel nods patiently. "I figured he would. And how was August fifteenth?"

She knows the weight that day holds.

"It was fine," I say, to my surprise. It's been a long time since I looked at that day with anything less than hostility. "It was... easier. I think that was thanks to Ocelle, too."

"Well, good."

Eventually, a bartender, a good-looking blonde girl, comes over. Annabel orders a martini, but I just take a gin and tonic and some sugar-coated peanuts. In no time, we have our drinks. Annabel stares into a glass that I would probably think was empty if not for the olive.

"Stars," she says suddenly, "I cannot fucking *stand* this shit."

"What, your drink? You can get another one. Here, on me."

"I'm not talking about the drink, dumbass." When she looks at me, her eyes are glazing over with annoyance. "I'm talking about... *this*. All of it. What's happened to all of us since the band fell apart. Nothing has been right since we got out of that fucking van."

I open my mouth to protest but fall silent. She's right, of course. So much has changed, and little has been for the better. I think of Kento's radio silence and Ocelle's flashy habits. The moths crawling all over the ceiling.

"What do you want me to do about it?" I ask, a little bitter. "Are you trying to be argumentative? It wasn't my fault that it all fell apart."

"Well, it wasn't mine either." She clenches her jaw and looks straight ahead, past the swinging lights to the large shelf of gin bottles behind the bar.

"Why'd you bring it up, then?" I press.

She hesitates now, and I see real pensive thought in the way her shoulders suddenly bunch up, the way her hands go white around her martini glass. "I don't know," she says tersely. "Maybe there's a tiny part of me that misses it. I don't know."

"Annabel, we can't go back."

"I know that," she snaps. "Don't you think I fucking know that?"

"We weren't happy when we were on tour."

She doesn't have a retort to this. She groans. I mean, it is an undebatable fact. We were so unhappy on tour, all of us, even Stan and Therese. The minutes we weren't yelling at each other were spent doped up, asleep, or both. I think I lost about ten pounds from all the stress.

"If we could figure out why we weren't so happy," Annabel finally ventures, "maybe we could fix it. Readjust some stuff."

"Well, that's the plan, right? We've been talking about getting back into the studio, recording the new album —"

"And then what?" she counters. "Things'll go back to the way they were? You, me, Kento, and Ocelle will just drop everything and tour the country again?"

"Why not? What are you getting at, man?"

"I'm saying," she says, "that something has to change if we don't want Mothic Wreckage to be a thing of the past. Another tour, exactly the way it was before, just won't work."

I start to feel a little woozy. The lights are too bright in here and the place smells strong, and I'm sure the gin and tonic isn't helping. I put a hand on the bar to steady myself. "So," I manage, "you're saying someone should leave the band."

"I don't think there's any other way to fix this," Annabel admits. "You know as well as I do. Someone has to go, and it's not gonna be either of us."

Kento or Ocelle. One has to go. The other can stay. Somehow I can't pick which one I'd prefer. Kento is so busy with his new EP, Ocelle is so... Ocelle. Having both of them is not an option.

"That's a hard problem to solve," I say.

"I know. And I don't think either of us can solve it right now. I think we have to be patient."

"Patient? How do you mean?"

"Let's just see how the next few months turn out," Annabel says. "See how Kento's EP does. If it bombs, he'll be on our doorstep in no time. If he turns out alright, then we can see if Ocelle is willing and able..."

"We'd have to watch him like a hawk."

"I know, I know." She holds up a conciliatory palm. "But I think that'll be our job either way, truthfully. How's he doing?"

I blink. I have been trying not to take note of how Ocelle is doing at all. When I come home from work most days, he is not doing anything particularly criminal, just sitting on the couch reading tarot cards or trying (and failing) to make a quiche. But even I, as ignorant as I try to be, can't ignore all the late nights out: him gone hours at a time, returning in a sweaty and giggly heap to bed in thin shirts and booty shorts, marks decorating his skin like freckles. He bottles himself up and then releases himself in batches too big for one person to stomach.

"I don't know," I eventually murmur.

Annabel blinks at me, no expression on her face. "You don't know," she repeats.

I shake my head. How do I even begin to explain this to her?

I must recover. "He's fine, I guess," I say. "I don't go out of my way to pay much attention. He's a grown man; I trust him."

She and I both know that none of this is true, but mercifully, she decides not to press me on any of it.

Outside the rain comes down in buckets, but the outdoor speakers are still playing oldies. I stand on the curb, drenched and woozy from the gin and tonic. My canvas shoes are soaked through. I don't quite know how I'm going to get home.

I wander. No one recognizes me in the rain. Through windows, I see teenagers studying hard in cafes, women holding babies, and a man quite like Ocelle fishing through a thrift store's collection of trinkets. I can't believe how unrecognizable I am. To be fair I look different now. My hair has lost so much of its blond color that it's almost brown again; I'm sure I'm thinner than I was. When I glance at my reflection in a passing shop window, I see my full form, as pathetic as it is. Pallid and sickly. My knuckles have gone gnarled and red, raw from tirelessly scrubbing the floor of Conan's bathroom. My clothes seem to dwarf me, my sleeves hanging to my fingertips.

I give myself uncanny valley.

Pretty soon I'm home again, after hailing a taxi and telling him to let me off at my complex's gate. Ocelle is repairing one of his sequined shirts, bedazzling it anew in places where the cloth has worn through. His journal sits open, covered with scribbles, on the other side of the couch.

"Did you have a nice time out?" he asks pleasantly, his eyes still on his work.

"Sure."

I don't tell him how much I worry about him. How my hands itch with anticipation, dreading that he will do something to himself any second. I want to scorn him.

I want to tell him *you're lucky, you know. I worry about you a lot more than I ought to.*

. . . .

The days continue blurring like pages in a stop motion, until one morning, I am listening to the radio at Conan's and a song from Kento's new EP comes on. Low and vital and rich.

Juniper and I stop working. Kento's voice, something I haven't heard often lately, is strong and clear. He sings about betrayal, about caring for someone who doesn't return the favor, and my tongue suddenly sits bitterly in my mouth. He is singing about Ocelle. His EP has come out, and the first song I've heard from it is about Ocelle.

"It's not bad," Juniper says contemplatively. "I kind of like it."

"No, it's really good," I agree. "Never thought it wouldn't be."

I pull out my phone and shoot Kento a text: *listening rn! so good man! congrats!*

He responds instantly: *thanks. i think we need to talk soon.*

Well, fuck. Fine. I text him back that I'd be happy to take him out to lunch and discuss some stuff, and even though my phone buzzes with his answer soon after, I stick it in my pocket and don't look. I return to my monotonous, blessed work, sticking price tags onto Paramore and Aqualung.

I am so caught up in what I am doing that I forget about Ocelle — and how he must be raging at home, throwing a temper tantrum over the radio.

TWENTY

The apartment is too quiet. Normally I'd walk in to see Ocelle having a solo dance party in the living room or clattering pans in the kitchen. Maybe taking photos of the sunset from out on the patio. Instead, the couch is gray and silent, the kitchen cold and unoccupied. The pale light from the setting winter sun outside the windows casts a dull sadness over the room: the feel of a space that is meant to be full of laughter and happiness but is not.

"Ocelle," I call out. My voice echoes in an answer, but otherwise, I hear nothing.

I peel my boots off and set my bag on the couch, moving through the apartment with slow socked feet. Ocelle can't have left. He wouldn't have left.

I peek down the hall, down to my open bedroom door. Ocelle is not asleep, but it looks like he has been, my covers all rumpled and chaotic. "Ocelle?" I say again, and a little noise like a whimper answers me from behind the closed bathroom door.

I come to a stop outside, resting my hand on the knob. "Ocelle, what's up?" I ask, as casually as I can.

"Nothing, starboy," he says from within, his voice clear and untroubled by worry. "I didn't know you'd be home so early."

"Can I come in?"

"No."

"Why not?"

He is quiet for a minute. "It's better if you don't," is the more hesitant reply.

"Ocelle."

"Yes?"

"I'm going to come in now."

His voice breaks. "Okay," he says.

I turn the knob and open the door to my bathroom. Outside the small dusty window, the cold light illuminates the ghost within. Ocelle is slumped against the tub wall, splayed out in one of my shirts and a pair of sweatpants and mismatched socks. His hair is pulled behind him into a messy ponytail. His eyes, dark and unfocused, are looking at the grout in the tile. His forehead glistens with sweat. In one limp hand, he holds a needle, his fingers quivering as they close around the vial.

I bend down in front of him and cup his cheek with my hand. "Oh, Ocelle," I murmur, "what have you done?"

He looks at me, his eyes still shifty and not quite right. Large circles underneath them create shadows on his cheeks. "I'm such a fucking piece of shit, Stars," he whispers. I can barely hear him over the tap, tap, tap of the dripping sink. "I went and I fucked it all up. The band, you and me, everything. I'm so sorry." For the first time in my life, I watch Ocelle break down into tears. He buries his face in his hands. "I'm so fucking sorry."

Wordlessly I gather him in my arms and settle him between my legs, his head leaning against my chest. My back is cold, flush with the tub wall. I take his hands in mine and look over the new bruises, flushing purple into the skin. It seems as though a gentle, sweet song plays from somewhere. I don't care. I don't feel like dancing. I am just content to sit here and hold Ocelle, sweet Ocelle, the one that maybe I can save, forever.

"I've got you," I say into his ear. The sound makes him shudder violently, his whole body trembling. "I'm not going anywhere."

Ocelle's body is racked with sobs. He is damp with sweat, but I keep my arms wrapped tightly around him anyway. "I'm so sorry," he says again. "I'm *so* sorry."

Even though I tell him to stop apologizing, he doesn't, and I hold him like that until well into the early hours of the morning. The moonlight pours in through the tiny window, illuminating his face, now motionless with sleep. Every time he exhales, I feel his breath on my neck. When he wakes, he'll be looking at me, if he remains at this angle.

"You know, you remind me so much of Cal," I murmur. Ocelle stirs but doesn't wake. "It's crazy sometimes. The way you tell jokes. You toss your head back when you laugh."

My voice is alien and odd, alone in this space. But even so, I keep talking.

"Cal was my everything," I say. "He was absolutely everything to me."

I close my eyes and lean my sore neck against the bathtub rim, imagining, for the millionth time, Cal's warm hands closing over my cold, shaky ones.

"I don't know what you'd call us." I scratch my cheek. "We weren't married, but we always pretended we were, so maybe we were, I don't know. No rings. No promises. Just us." The memory tastes bittersweet in my mouth. "We lived here, real quiet. And then, one day, I don't know. He got sick, and the rest happened pretty quickly." I run a hand through Ocelle's curly mop of hair, laughing a little to myself. "It was actually about a month or two. That's how late they found it. So it was more like, 'Okay, yeah, this dude's gonna die. Say your goodbyes 'cause it could end tomorrow.'"

I don't remember much of that month. Just him searching for me in the dark during those last couple of days, asking for Mothic Wreckage the same way he'd plead for water, with parched lips and an empty, arid throat.

As I am telling Ocelle this, sitting on our bathroom floor, I feel a heavy weight rising from my shoulders. I have never said any of this out loud, only repeated it in my brain over and over infinitely, looking for loopholes and places I took the wrong step. Even though Ocelle doesn't know it, I like to think I bared my soul all the same.

• • • •

I don't think there's any other way to say it. I am unhappy.

Every morning I wake before Ocelle. I make sure that his usual hiding spots are empty (he was forced to give them to me, of course). I feel like a mother childproofing a dangerous room in the house. Knives are hidden away. I threw out all the liquor on Monday. I'm trying my best.

After my perfunctory patrol of the apartment, I leave before Ocelle even wakes — leaving him a pastry and some hot chocolate in the kitchen — and drive to work. I sweep and tag and drink lukewarm soda while the radio blares Kento's music, my stomach churning endlessly with doubt and worry. I spend most of my time daydreaming. My mind is the only place where anything makes sense.

After work, sometimes I'll see someone: Lily, maybe, out to dinner (her treat since I can't pay) or Cal's twin sister, Camilla, who moved back into town recently after finishing her degree at Stanford. Annabel becomes a rare face, Kento even rarer, and Stan and Therese unheard of. Ocelle is an interesting enough conversation to have but sometimes, when I come home, I can barely look him in the eye. I don't know if it's shame or pity or frustration. I don't know if maybe it's because I want to take his face in my hands and kiss it, over and over and over again, never pausing to think.

So for the most part I am alone. I spend the most time with myself, which is an unfortunate companion for me to have, especially given my mood lately. Maybe it'll be productive, I think halfheartedly. I'm not a good songwriter at all, but all our biggest hits came to me when I was depressed. I don't know if that's good or bad.

There is one day when I'm not quite so alone, but again, the pros and cons of this can be debated; while I am taking my lunch break at Conan's, sitting in my car alone with the heat going, my dad calls me.

I stare at my phone as it rings in my cup holder, nonplussed. I don't think I've heard my dad's voice in about five years.

Tentatively I pick up. For a moment I hear nothing but my breathing. "Hello?" I venture.

My dad's voice is quick and sharp, official and businesslike, as if we spoke last week. He has always talked too fast. "Stars. Yes. Hello. How are you?"

I can't think of a thing to say. Making up with Violet was one thing. My father is worse.

"I'm fine," I stammer. "Uh... how are you?"

"Fine, thank you." A pause. "Someone has reached out to me. They said you were quite unwell."

"Unwell?"

"I've heard things have been hard lately."

"Well, sure," I say, trying to keep the sarcasm out of my voice. "But they haven't been that bad. Not bad enough for it to come back to you, that's for certain."

My dad doesn't say anything for a while. When I was estranged from my family, shortly after graduating high school — for a myriad of reasons — it was mostly my mother at the helm, dragging my father along behind her like an obedient dog. Even so, it had been made clear that no one was on my side, not even my sisters.

"Stars," my dad finally says, "please come home and let us help you." "No."

"Please." His voice suggests to me that maybe my refusal is more than he can bear. "I need you. We *need* you. We need to know that you're alright."

I remember my mother saying the same thing, back at Yndo that one afternoon. For a painstaking, splitting second, I almost say yes. Yes, I'll come home, yes, I'll come back. But when I close my eyes and take a breath, I remember Ocelle, how pathetic he'd looked, twitching on the floor of the bathroom. My heart twists with pity.

"I can't," I hear myself murmur. "I have Violet. I'm fine."

"Stars —"

"Thanks for calling." I hang up.

Who had reached out to him? I wonder. He'd said that someone had told him what was wrong with me. It couldn't have been anyone from the band; they knew very little, if anything, about either of my parents. Violet wouldn't do that to me. It couldn't have been Lily, either. Sure, she knew my family, but she would never.

Thinking about it, I take the mop from the back room of Conan's and resume my travails.

amilla asks me to meet her for lunch the following Saturday. I warn her that I can't pay for much, but she waves that off. She's got a big fancy degree now, she reminds me, and she can treat me.

When I walk in, I immediately spot her and sit across from her. She and Cal look nothing alike — she is blonde, his hair was brown, her eyes are blue, his were hazel — but if you sat them side by side there'd be no denying that they were siblings. It's overwhelming to look at Camilla. All of Cal's little mannerisms, all of his quirks that I spent so much time trying to memorize, suddenly replicated perfectly, right in front of me.

Camilla smiles at me and I almost fall apart right then and there. It is too painfully familiar, it just is.

"Thanks for meeting me," she says.

"Sure. It was about time we got together again."

She snorts. "Well, it's only been about a week."

"Still."

"How are you?" she asks.

I don't know how to answer her. I shrug. "I've been worse."

Something tugs at Camilla's well-meaning grin; her shoulders slump a little as she flips through the menu, which is all hot dogs and burgers and shakes. "Yeah," she mutters. "I figured."

"It's fine, though. I'll get through it."

"I know you will." She blows some hair out of her face. Her jean jacket is too big for her. "We both will, it's just..."

"Hard," I finish.

"Right."

Over the speakers, *Flyday Chinatown* is playing — interesting choice. Ocelle likes that song.

Camilla, to my surprise, reaches across the table and takes both of my hands in hers. Her fingers are warm and soft, unlike my mother's.

She has a little tattoo right underneath her thumb: a C. I've never asked who it's for, her or Cal. She'd tell me if she wanted me to know. Her wedding band glitters thinly; my mouth runs dry, sad. I don't like rings. I had been thinking about getting Cal a ring.

"How's Huck?" I ask, my eyes still on Camilla's fingers. Huck's her husband, a pretty standup guy.

"Good," she says. "He sends his love."

"And Harvey?" Cal and Camilla's younger brother — he'd been about eighteen when everything had happened.

"Harv's good. He says hi."

"Thanks. Return the favor."

"Sure."

Silence floods again, and we look at each other. Camilla knits her eyebrows, concerned. She cups my cheek in her palm.

"Please tell me you're taking care of yourself," she says quietly. "I can't lose you too."

I grab her bony wrist with a cold hand. "Yeah. I know. I'm fine."

"Do you promise?"

"Yes."

She remains unconvinced, but she nods. She brushes her thumb against my jaw lovingly, like a sister, and her hand retreats into her lap.

· · · ·

Annabel has another gig: a bigger one, better than ever. Finally, she seems to have listened to us and realized her worth, because she's not an opener but the main act. And not at some tiny little joint like Rigby's either: it's at the Mercury, the biggest club in the city. We've played there once or twice as Mothic Wreckage, so it's nothing new, but it's still a massive deal. When you're on that stage, especially alone, with the whole of the club looking at you, you feel like Zeus.

I almost missed the last one entirely, and I can't even begin to think of missing another one, so I make doubly sure I'm not busy. Friday

night. The Mercury. Doors open at eight. I will be there. Ocelle and
Lily, too, the whole family. I should shop for something nice to wear. I
don't have many nice clothes to go partying in, and I am too proud to
ask to borrow one of Ocelle's silky shirts. I send Lily a text, asking her
if there's anything in her closet I can borrow, and she shoots back immediately with a proposal: let's both go shopping together tomorrow
afternoon. We both need new clothes anyway.

It ends up being a little bit more difficult than I imagined to find
things that fit me. I haven't bought clothes for myself in a long time —
since before Cal died, even — and I'm not used to the way that price
tags feel in my hands, the way that lint collects in the corners of fitting
room floors, chairs sitting by mirrors with little kids' footprints. Lily
does most of the work, picking things that she thinks I'd look nice in
with a carefree "yeah, that'll do" and tossing them into the pile in my
arms. Occasionally she'll see something that she wants and fold it over
her arm lovingly, smoothing out creases.

When I try on the clothes Lily picked out and look at myself in the
mirror, it's as if I don't belong to my own body. I seem all at once to be
quite short and quite tall, wide and thin, in the satin blouse, the leather
jacket, and the dark pants. I clench my jaw as I study myself. I look like
a Greek god. I look like Ocelle.

"Do you like 'em?" I hear Lily ask from just outside the fitting room
door.

"Yes," I say, and start to undo the lace-covered snaps. "I don't know
how much I can afford, but these are good to start."

I open the door once I'm done changing and Lily beams at me, happy as a little kid, her arms full of clothes.

"I'm glad you liked what I picked," she says earnestly. "You should
wear that to the gig, it'll be great. Ocelle is just gonna *die* over you."

"Oh, stop." I step through the doorway, holding the knob for her.
"Your turn."

I sit outside the fitting room and wait, doing some puzzles on my phone to pass the time. Lily takes quite a while, longer than normal. I sit, as awkward as ever, among the other girls, who all flit past holding dresses and blouses, shooting curious, disgusted glimpses at me. I see Lily's socked feet moving underneath the door, but she still doesn't emerge.

When the place quiets a little, I say, "Lily, is everything okay?"

Her anxious little feet in their fuzzy socks stop moving. "Can you come in here?" she asks softly.

"In — in there? With you?"

"Yeah."

I stand and brush off my shirt, dusty with lint from around the room. "Sure."

When I push on the door, it opens easily, and I step inside. Lily is leaning against the opposite mirror, teary-eyed, with flushed cheeks. Her clothes are in a heap on the floor. Outside, other people giggle and chatter as they try on their items, but here, Lily is crying and I don't know why.

She gestures to her stomach, where the denim shorts that she is currently trying on do not button all the way. "They're too small," she says. I can barely hear her. "They're my normal size. But they're too small."

I reach out and brush a tear off her cheek. "So what? Go up a size. There's no shame in that."

I didn't say it to be mean, but Lily hugs her middle and cries. She looks so truly unhappy, all because of a button that won't fasten.

I pull her close, and she sobs into my shirt.

For a long time, we stand there like that. Lily cries on me and I look past the top of her head, making eye contact with myself in the mirror. Her girlish, scraped knees tremble. Outside, I hear other people continue to have fun — someone shrieks with laughter.

"Lily," I say. "Let's get you the next size up — no shame in it, nothing wrong with that — and let's head out, okay? This place is depressing."

She sniffles and leans back from me, rubbing at her waterline. "I bet my makeup's all runny now," she mumbles. "Serves me right for being such a dramatic bitch."

"Don't say that. We can fix it, come on."

"I don't know."

"Come on," I say again, taking her hand. "Annabel would hate to see you like this. She'll probably get onto me for letting it happen at all."

"I'm not a child," Lily says indignantly.

I don't answer. Instead, I help her gather her things and lead her out of the fitting room, back to the rack where these cursed denim shorts had come from. Lily, sighing, leafs through the remaining pairs of cutoffs and finds ones in the next size, exchanging them for the old ones.

In the car she explains it to me. Eating her feelings. All those bakery dates with Annabel start to pile up. Why? I ask — she seems happy enough. And she says she is happy enough, truly, but she misses Cal and her parents and the way things used to be. She misses seeing *me* happy. She's nostalgic for a time she barely remembered.

I hold her hand between the seats of the car. "I know what that's like," I say softly. "I know it all too well."

Sighing, she kisses me on the cheek.

All in all, I'd call it a sad afternoon.

· · · ·

Annabel's set is not as good as it was before. She plays with less intention, less heat. Between songs her face only betrays the fact that she's anxious, not grateful or excited or relieved, even, to be back on the main stage. We clap for her all the same, me and Lily (in her slightly bigger shorts) and Ocelle, all of us a little semicircle of encouragement right at the base of the stage. If Annabel hears our applause, she does not make it known. She studies the crowd with worried, fretful glances, chewing on her lower lip, her hands trembling over her ukulele.

I lean over and ask Lily. "Why's she so nervous?"

She blinks at me. "I can't hear you," she says loudly over the music.

Impatiently I pull out my phone and text her. *i said why is she so nervous?*

Lily looks at her phone screen, then back at me, and shrugs.

After the set, when the four of us are walking to dinner at The Rouge, I get up the courage to ask Annabel myself.

"It was really good..." I preface, testing the waters.

She doesn't look at me. She only clenches her jaw and stares straight ahead in that familiar Annabel way. "Thanks."

"...but is everything okay?"

Her grip tightens on the strap of her bag. Lily winces as if Annabel is holding her hand too tight.

"I'm fine," she grumbles.

"Are you sure?"

"I'm fine!" she says again, angrier this time. She wrestles herself away from Lily and turns to look at us all with a venomous glare. "Don't you people fucking get it? I'm *fine*. I'm great. My life is perfect. Beautiful fucking girlfriend, I'm a damn good musician, people *love* me...fuck." She runs a hand through her hair, stressed, looking out at the neon lights in the street. They create a red glistening in her bright eyes that turns green when the cars begin to move again. "I'm *perfect*. I have a perfect life. Why the fuck am I so unhappy?"

I used to echo something of the same sentiment.

I wish I could tell her that. Instead, Ocelle and Lily and I watch as she wipes her eyes, turns, and stomps down the sidewalk. When she should turn to reach the restaurant, she instead turns to go home, and not a single one of us stops her.

"She misses the band," Lily translates.

"Yeah, don't we all, toots," Ocelle says, yawning.

"I don't understand." I shift my stance. "She's doing fine on her own."

Lily looks out into the street, where clumps of young people are laughing and talking. "It's complicated," she says. "It's better with other people."

Ocelle nods like this is some sort of profound statement. He wraps his arms around me and squeezes, tight. "Alright, altar of heaven. Let's go home."

So we do. The whole route there, I'm thinking about Annabel, and what Lily had said: *it's better with other people.* Is it? For Kento it wasn't. But Annabel loved Mothic Wreckage, probably more than any of us.

It doesn't seem fair that we wrestled it out of her grasp.

TWENTY-TWO

Y ou're going to dislike me for this. Telling the story this way, I mean. There's something I can't deny about how I'm telling it: somewhat distantly, like I'm looking through an old photo album with you. I think the truth is that adding the tenderness that drenched everything during this time is hard to do. Difficult to bear, but for you, I'll do it. I know you can take it.

Annabel does not talk to us for a while. Lily falls similarly silent. Kento's nowhere to be found — although rumors are he might go on a solo tour — so that leaves me and Ocelle, sitting on our couch, eating ramen in silence.

How could I force you to bear this sweetness with me? The way he'd draw his legs against his chest, lean his chin against his knee as the TV blares *L.A. Law* or *Gilligan's Island*. How we'd look at each other when we thought the other was not paying attention. How we went to bed with miles and miles of space between us, me with an achy back and creaking neck on the couch and him, warm and soft and small in my sheets. How every morning I woke to a tall glass of apricot juice on the coffee table, and how every morning I just couldn't get up the courage to tell him how much I hate apricot juice.

You will hate me for this. I know you will. Truthfully I don't know how else to tell it.

One afternoon, I am painting on Cal's old easel, which I dug out of the garage. I run my hands over the little paint splotches he left behind, tasting each one, remembering them on my tongue. I sit by the open window in the bedroom, painting under all the curtains of beaded glass, while Ocelle fiddles with my keyboard, flush against the opposite wall. He plays the opening chords of one of Chopin's etudes, then stops, his fingers faltering.

"Any requests?" he asks softly.

I dip my brush again and add a violent, hasty flush of pink to the skin of the old man I am drawing. "Play me something nice," I say. "Something I'll like."

Ocelle wordlessly begins the theme song to *All Quiet on the Western Front*.

"Maybe *Interstellar*," I suggest.

He blends the notes and then, a moment later, boom — he is playing *Interstellar*.

I smile to myself as I blend out the pink, back into the beige. "La Campanella," I suggest next.

"Fuck you," Ocelle says, and continues to play.

It makes me laugh, really laugh, for the first time in a long while. I stop mid-brush stroke and laugh, and the music ceases.

I turn to look at Ocelle, who is staring at me. "Why'd you stop?" I ask. "It was wonderful. Keep going."

He doesn't answer for a moment. He blinks, and then his face blooms into a smile. A genuine smile.

"I've missed that," he says. "I missed your silly little laugh. Silly and clear as a bell."

A peaceful silence fills the room. Eventually, we both go back to our work, me with the brushes and him on the keys. Who's the piano man now?

"You know what I think we should do," Ocelle says, now gently plucking out a soft, lilting melody, "quite urgently, and with little to no prep?"

That's never good. "What?"

"Let's go visit my parents."

It takes me so by surprise that I dip my brush into my cup of coffee instead of my paint water. I have never, for as long as I have known Ocelle, known anything about his parents. He has never mentioned them, I have never met them after a show — the only clue that I had to indicate he'd had any parents at all was that damned orange blanket, now wadded in a sad ball and tossed to the end of the bed.

"Your parents?" I repeat, hesitating. "You want to go see your parents?"

"Yes." There's something of amusement in Ocelle's voice. "They've got a farm, just across the state line, and I think I'd like to go see them. It's about time you met them, anyway."

"I always thought you were..."

"What? Estranged?"

"Something like that."

"No," he says airily. "Just mutually uninterested."

So it's decided. Ocelle phones his mother that night and asks for permission to come to visit that weekend; I don't hear her voice, but Ocelle grins wide, and I know the proposition has been accepted.

That's how I ended up driving to Kansas on Friday afternoon, Ocelle in the seat next to me with the AUX cord in hand and the window rolled down. It blows his scent towards me, familiar and invited and welcomed. He doesn't say much during the drive, just looks out at the passing fields.

"It's like we're back on tour," he says at one point.

"Ha. Yeah."

Quiet again. "Do you miss it?"

"Sometimes. Do you?"

He looks at me and smiles like I'm another adorable fan asking for a photo. "More than anything in the world," he says.

• • • •

This is not where I'd pictured Ocelle growing up. I knew he'd come from Kansas, but I didn't know that meant this, all sunflower plots and peeling wood. The farm is ugly and small, rotten and hollow, with dying azalea shrubs and a single, lonely-looking old horse grazing behind a watershed. I park in the only unoccupied slot in an otherwise busy driveway, and we hop out, our bags over our shoulders.

It must have been hard to make friends out here.

"Home sweet home," Ocelle announces. "Haven't been here since before my twentieth birthday, can you believe that?"

"Yes," I say, looking around. If I'd been Ocelle I would have wanted to leave as soon as possible too.

We trek across one of the fields, fighting off chiggers and ticks until we reach the house, which is a lot uglier up close. The panels of windows are missing. The screen door is open, peppered with holes. The front door is open, too, and someone inside is clanking pots and pans together. Ah, so it's genetic. That's how Ocelle knows how to be so loud in my kitchen.

"I'm home," Ocelle says as we step through the threshold. "I know you all missed me *so* much."

I scooch in after him, a little bit scared of what might be on the other side. A lot of family photos — though none of Ocelle, just of two parents and a little girl — and fishing trophies. Two degrees from the same community college. To our right is a living room where, on the TV, renowned wilderness expert Nico Osgood is teaching us how to build a fire without using flint and steel. In a great big armchair, moth-eaten and sagging off its skeleton, is an older man. Even though he is old and scraggly and sour-looking, there can't be any mistaking that he is Ocelle's father. They hold their heads the same way, study what has their attention with relish as if eating up every detail under some intense time limit.

When Ocelle steps through the door and announces his entrance, his father looks at us, and his expression doesn't change.

"Adam," he says to Ocelle. "Man, I didn't think you'd come."

"It's Ocelle," Ocelle corrects him breezily, moving to kiss him on the cheek.

"You're dressed like a damned fairy."

"Thank you." Ocelle stands back up and gestures for me to follow him. I let him lead me into the kitchen, where a woman — again, the parentage is unmistakable — washes dishes with coarse, raw hands. She looks up, startled as a pigeon, when we come in.

"Oh," she says, putting her current dish down and wiping her hands on her dress. "I didn't... sorry. I didn't know you'd be coming before noon."

"We made good time," Ocelle says politely.

His mother takes a few hesitating steps toward Ocelle and reaches out, as if afraid to touch him. Maybe he will disappear if he is touched. She puts her fingers in his curly hair and laughs a little as if she can't believe he's real.

I know that feeling.

"Your hair has gotten so long," she says.

"I know. Isn't it great?"

To my surprise, his mother's eyes blur with tears. "I've missed you, Adam," she says softly.

"It's Ocelle," Ocelle says again, with no change in his bubbly expression or tone.

"Ocelle," she concedes, pulling her hand back. Then her eyes fall on me, and she wipes at her lower lids. "Oh, sorry. I'm being rude. This is Stars, right?"

"Yep," Ocelle says. "Y'know, the real-life Astro Boy. The frontrunner of the late-once-great Mothic Wreckage."

"I'd be a fool not to know all that." His mother holds out her hand to me. "Amaya Galler. A pleasure to finally meet you."

"It's an honor," I say, trying not to stumble over my words as our hands connect. She shakes mine heartily, with a grip I wouldn't expect from a woman of her stature.

"Where's Zee?" Ocelle asks, batting his eyelashes.

"Upstairs. You're welcome to go say hi."

"Alright. Then we're off to do that."

"I'll have lunch ready in about an hour," Amaya says as we're leaving.

Ocelle leads me upstairs by the hand. We pass more photos, bugs encased in glass, a photo of two men — one tall, mustached, the other small and friendly-looking — in front of a forest, thumbs up and smiles abound. Only one photo of Ocelle is here that I can see, of him and a young girl on a picnic blanket surrounded by trees. But that's the only one.

When we reach the second floor of the house, the wood creaking beneath our feet, I say: "Adam Galler? That's your name?"

Ocelle turns to look at me, the usual friendly light in his eyes now quite gone. "No," he says flatly. "My name is Ocelle. I expect you to remember."

His tone makes me shift uncomfortably, creating more noise against the floorboards. "Right. Sorry."

Ocelle turns again without saying anything — without letting me off the hook, his favorite way to tease — and leads me to a door at the end of the hall. He raps on it twice.

"Go away," someone — a girl — says from within.

"No," Ocelle says back. "You know how long we drove to get here? Come out."

Silence. Just enough time passes for me to think that whoever sits on the other side has continued to ignore Ocelle — but then the door opens, and a young girl appears, maybe fifteen or sixteen, with Ocelle's most striking features. That's the girl from the photo. It takes me by surprise. If Ocelle were a girl — I mean, more than he is now — he'd look exactly like this.

The girl looks at Ocelle, then me, then back at Ocelle. "Oh," she says, leaning in for an awkward side hug. "They... didn't tell me you were coming."

"It was an impulsive trip," Ocelle says. He turns to me. "Stars, this is my younger sister. Zita-Mae."

Zita-Mae rolls her eyes. "Oh, God," she grumbles. "Call me Zee, please. I'm fucking begging you."

I introduce myself to her too, but she doesn't take my hand when I hold it out to her. She ushers us inside and closes the door behind her.

Her room is cool. She has a hamster cage in one corner, the bed shoved in the other as if sleep doesn't matter all that much. She is just like Ocelle. Her curtains are lace and her sheets are silk. Her desk is littered with papers: receipts, notes from friends, and looseleaf homework. Over her bed are posters for Jimmy Eat World, Melanie Martinez, and — wouldn't you know it — Mothic Wreckage.

Our limited edition vinyl is on her floor, flipped to the B-side.

Ocelle and I sit on the edge of her bed (her comforter has strawberries on it) while she sits in her desk chair, spinning around.

"You've gotten taller," Ocelle says.

"Well, yeah, no shit. It's been like five years."

This makes Ocelle go quiet. "I meant to come back," he says haughtily, as if this solves everything. "Just never got around to it. Too busy living the rockstar life, y'know."

"Well, until the band fell to pieces, that was probably a pretty good excuse," Zee says.

Ocelle sighs and flops over dramatically onto her bed. "I see the attitude has grown right alongside the girl."

"That's what happens when you dip for half a decade."

"Okay," I say, standing quite suddenly. "I'm gonna, uh, I'm gonna go. This seems like a private thing."

"No, no," Ocelle says, waving his hand like he can't be bothered to get up and chase after me. "Sit. Theatricality runs in the family, I'm afraid."

"So does the fun of being thoughtful. If you'd come back every once in a while, we'd know how you were doing," Zee grumbles, scribbling on the cuff of her jeans with a paint marker. I crane my neck to see what she is drawing: lotus blossoms, over and over, the pink cutting thick into the denim.

"Fine. I should have come back. You win." Ocelle winks at her without smiling. "I've missed you, kid. Lighten up a little."

Zee just sighs and rolls her eyes, but I see a grin tug at the corners of her small mouth.

That night at dinner, the awkward silence is as thick as a blackout curtain, creating a spreading chasm where the dining room table should have been. Ocelle and I on one end, Mr. Galler and Amaya on the other, and Zee at the head of the table, regal as a queen. The food is alright, but the conversation is awful. I know, I know, beautiful and divine Ocelle is usually working wonders in any conversation, but now he just sits and serenely picks at his macaroni and cheese, vaguely disinterested.

"So, Stars," Mr. Galler says. "What are you doing now that, uh, Mothic Wreckage is over? Any new, uh, creative endeavors?"

"Sure," I stammer, taken aback by the sudden rush of attention from the rest of the table. "Well, uh..." I am truly at a loss for what to say. I make eye contact with Ocelle, and he gives me a knowing look. *Don't mention the possibility of the band getting back together. I will never hear the end of it.* "I'm working on some solo music," I say, lying out of my ass, "so I'll hopefully be coming out with my first independent album by January."

"That's lovely," Amaya says politely.

"And, uh —" Mr. Galler turns his gaze to Ocelle, but can only look for a split second before returning to his mac and cheese. "And what about you, Ad — Ocelle?"

Ocelle shrugs, playing with the tines on his fork. "Right now I'm living with Stars and making his life hell," he says peacefully, "but sooner or later I'll get a job and be out of his hair. Get an apartment somewhere, maybe adopt a stray dog, you know how I am."

Amaya shifts uncomfortably in her seat, and the silence ensues once more as if it had never gone.

This is how the rest of the dinner does: Ocelle, guzzling white wine, not saying much — and the rest of us are not in a massive hurry to compensate. After dinner, Zee turns on some old movie in the living room to watch with Mr. Galler, and Amaya starts on the dishes. Ocelle leads me back to his childhood bedroom, swaying, woozy from the wine.

"What do you think?" he asks, spreading out his hands. "Do you think it looks like my kind of room?"

It is dusty and mostly unoccupied. An old bedframe with turned-down sheets, worn through. The bookshelf is empty and dusty. The desk fares similarly. A couple of things remain on the wall, though: some photos of a much younger Ocelle with other people I'd never seen before. Four girls, all surrounding him like a posse in the middle of a middle school hallway.

Ocelle sees me looking. He points sluggishly at each girl. "That's Claire. And Elle. That's Milena, that's Holly. They were my best friends in the whole world. Well, until you."

"Shucks."

He nods and focuses on the bed. "It'll be a tight fit," he says. "I'll just take the floor if you don't want to be so cramped all night."

"It's fine," I say, maybe too quickly. "We'll manage."

He smiles at me in a way that tells me he wouldn't have had it any other way.

TWENTY-THREE

I n the middle of the night, Ocelle rolls over and puts a cold hand on my shoulder, shaking me awake. "Stars. It's time. Get up."

"What?" I ask blearily, rubbing the sleep out of my eyes. My stomach dimly flashes with panic; this is what had happened before, with Cal. I hate being woken in the middle of the night. I urge myself to calm and be still; this isn't like Cal. That's not happening. That's over.

"Get up," Ocelle insists again, swatting me lightly with the pillow as he hops out of the bed. "We've got something to do, you and I."

"Will you stop being cryptic and please tell me what the fuck —?"

"No. C'mon."

When I blink again he is gone and the bathroom light is on. I stumble in, still half-asleep. He is in front of the mirror, studying his face intently, wearing nothing but briefs and flannel and mismatched socks.

"What are you doing?" I half-whine. "It's so early."

He reaches into the sink drawer and pulls out a razor, plugging it into the wall. "You're going to help me with something."

"Huh?"

He turns towards me fully now and holds the razor out at arm's length. "Shave," he orders.

I blink at him, not quite sure I heard him correctly.

"*Shave*," he says again. "Cut my hair off. Right now."

I take the razor in my hand and study it. It buzzes lowly. "Shave?" I repeat, the word sounding about as Greek and unfamiliar as they come. "Shave your hair?"

"That's what I said."

"Why?"

"For fuck's sake, will you please just fucking do it?"

Still reeling, I come behind him and put my hands on his shoulders. "Are — are you sure?"

"Positive, baby. Have at it."

As if it were some sort of ceremonial ritual, I find the first lock of hair and cut through it, letting the curls fall to the tile floor by our feet. Ocelle stares at himself in the mirror, blank-faced, as I get rid of the hair that's captivated so many over the years. Myself included.

Gently I take away one tress, then another. I am careful not to hurt Ocelle's ears. I brush off the nape of his neck whenever there is no way to see what I am doing. After a while, when I am mostly finished with the back, I tell Ocelle to face me and hop onto the sink itself, which he does. We stare at each other while I work, cutting his curly flower of hair into a sharp buzz. I brush loose strands off his cheeks, off his lips. When I am done, we stand surrounded by a sea of brown hair, long and luscious and beautiful, and in front of me is one of the most beautiful people I have ever seen.

I put the razor down and flick it off. "I'm done," I murmur, raising my hand to his face and swiping away one last stray piece. "I'm finished."

Ocelle, in response, only smiles, looking relieved. He reaches out, too, and finds my cheek in his palm. Tenderly, as if he's waited all his life to do it, he pulls my head closer to his and kisses me. I taste the white wine he had at dinner. He hasn't brushed his teeth. I don't dare pull away.

When we're done, Ocelle's hands tracing over my shoulders, he leaves his lips a centimeter away from my neck.

"I love you, Stars," he says, just loud enough for me to hear. The sound of his voice is clear, now unobstructed by hair. "I love you more than just about anything."

I lean into his embrace. He buries his face in my shoulder, and I make eye contact with myself in the mirror.

"Aster," I say softly.

"Hmm?"

"My —" I can barely hear myself over the sound of my heart breaking. "My name's Aster."

I expect him to tell me, yes, Stars is better, yes, no wonder you've never told me before, blah blah blah. Instead, he sits back up and looks at me again — adoringly.

"Aster," Ocelle says. "That suits you."

We quietly laugh together.

· · · ·

Ocelle ends up regretting cutting all his hair off. He doesn't say so explicitly, but you can tell by the way he runs his hand over the shady buzz, a dissatisfied look on his face, like he feels something is missing but not quite where it went. Zee tells him he looks like an army cadet; Mr. Galler says he looks more like a statue of an old Roman soldier. Amaya denies commenting much, keeping her eyes fixed on her lasagna-stained dishes in the sink.

On our third afternoon at the Galler farm, Kento calls.

My phone rings and I pick it up. "Hi, Kento. Where've you been?"

"Can I talk to Ocelle?" he asks without much pomp. "He has me blocked on his cell."

"Sure," I say, startled. "Uh, let me go get him. Is everything okay?"

"Yes. Fine. I'd just really like to talk to him."

"Okay," I murmur, and slip out the door and into the living room, where Ocelle is balancing a charcuterie board on his lap. In one hand is a cracker; in the other is a joint, ablaze. I think he's been re-reading old letters that he found in his room because his keepsake box is on the rocking chair. I hold out my phone to him. "It's for you. It's Kento."

Ocelle blinks at me, his mouth full of cheese.

"Take it," I insist. Ocelle puts his cracker down and grabs the phone.

I head upstairs to give them some space. Behind her closed door, I can hear Zee playing a song from our first album. One of the most tedious ones to sing at concerts, thanks to that high B flat. I cringe at the memory and shuffle back into our room, where I collapse face-first on the bed, smelling the mildewy old curtains and pillowcases.

Ocelle doesn't come up for a long time. I work on my laptop for a while, messaging Lily and Annabel — but, respectfully, leaving Kento and Ocelle on their own. I stalk my own Facebook profile, heading into the deep recesses of my photo albums to look at all the memories I've accumulated over the years. Some with Cal, some not. Some with Ocelle, some not. All with me stuck square in the middle, never entirely content.

I drift off to sleep, and when I wake again, it is because Ocelle is standing over me, phone in hand. He startles me at first; I'm still not used to his hair, or lack thereof.

"Hey," I say as I sit, rubbing my eyes. "How'd your call with Kento go?"

Ocelle blinks, his face blank. Then his mouth spreads into a victorious smile. "He apologized," he says. "He called to apologize."

"To... apologize?"

"Mhm." Ocelle reaches over and turns the bedside lamp on. His face is now illuminated like a ghost, and he begins to gesticulate, telling the story. "He said that I've come such a long way from where I was, and the band should never have fallen apart because of what happened between us. He apologized for what happened to Mothic Wreckage, and he apologized for butting into my business."

I gape at him. "No, he didn't."

"Are you calling me a liar?" Ocelle asks, light but a trifle sharp. He hops over onto the bed next to me. "That's exactly what he said. He said, 'Sorry for everything. Congrats on getting clean.'"

I have to laugh. "You're not clean," I mutter.

Ocelle doesn't answer me. He looks out the window at the fields, cornstalks billowing gently in the dark. "I'm trying," is his final, faint reply. He picks at the remnants of a scab on the inside of his forearm. "I haven't in a while."

"I know."

Ocelle looks at me, opens his mouth like he'll say something else, but falls silent. Quickly he leans over and kisses me before diving under the covers and turning away from me, closing his eyes.

TWENTY-FOUR

We leave the Galler farm the next lazy morning, quite unexpectedly. Ocelle randomly decides that he needs to go home, and that's why we leave. He gives Zee a feathery little hug but neglects to touch either of his parents. Amaya pulls me in close and murmurs something about "please take care of him," patting me on the back with the flats of her hands. Mr. Galler gives me a firm handshake, his skin stretching thinly and translucent over his knobby knuckles.

And then we're on the road again.

"Is that really what Kento said to you?" I ask, turning the radio down.

Ocelle turns the radio back up. Message received loud and clear.

The drive back is much less pleasant than the one before. We don't talk. We don't hold hands. My foot remains pressed against the gas the whole time. We don't pass a single car for the first few hours. We must be the only people that exist on this skinny stretch of Kansas interstate.

Ocelle leans out the window. He sticks his tongue out at passing farmhouses, abandoned silos, and lone herds of cows. He looks less like himself without all the hair, but he doesn't look bad. Just smaller.

Defiantly he juts his chin out at a lonely-looking billboard for a barber's shop. "I won't cut my hair again until it rains," he says to me proudly. "It's not like I'd have much to cut anyway."

For the rest of the way home, he sings along to the radio. He's memorized every damn chord of every damn song, and I adore him for it.

And when we cross the border, Ocelle looks back at the *Welcome to Colorado* sign and says to me with a wicked grin, "Toto, I've a feeling we're not in Kansas anymore."

"Aren't you funny," I deadpan.

His socked feet appear on the dash. "Did your dad ever call you?"

"What?"

"Your dad. He ever reach out?"

My hands go cold on the steering wheel. "It was you?" I ask.

He doesn't answer. In the mirror I see him smile.

"What the fuck, Ocelle?" I grumble. "That was so not your problem."

"Everything's my problem."

"That's bullshit."

"I was trying to help," Ocelle says, his nose in the air. "I know what it's like to hate your dad's guts. I don't want that for you."

"That's something I don't need your help with."

"Whatever."

The car goes silent for a few miles.

"I really was just trying to help," Ocelle says again. "You seemed so upset all the time. The type of upset that parents are really good at."

I chew on his words. "If you were really trying to help me, it was misguided."

"You've made that much clear."

"Thanks anyway," I mutter. "I see where you were coming from."

I don't look at him, and he doesn't look at me, but I feel a loving hand appear on my thigh.

· · · ·

When we get home and toss our stuff on the couch, something has changed. Outside the sun has long set. We are at a standstill, looking at each other in the dark living room. Reminiscing over what could have been — and what has yet to be.

"Stars," Ocelle says. "Kento did apologize to me. You can believe something else if you'd like."

"I believe you," I say. I still don't know if I do.

He nods. "Okay."

"I don't believe he congratulated you on being clean."

"No, he didn't do that," Ocelle admits. "But he applauded my efforts."

"That was nice of him."

Ocelle hesitates before he speaks again. "Stars. I have something to ask you."

"Okay."

"Are you proud of me?"

I step forward and take his hands, kissing his palms. "I could never be prouder."

He smiles at me. A big, bright, beautiful smile in the dim living room. That's all he wanted me to say.

We head back to bed together, and he takes me like a chess piece.

It feels like holding your breath and releasing it all the same. I claw my way through the fabric of Ocelle's shirt, toss it onto the carpeted floor, and then we are pressed together. Two bodies in the dark. For the first time since I lost Cal, I let myself inhale, and for the first time since I met Ocelle, I let myself exhale. I feel whole again. My eyes blur with tears. I smile. I feel *whole* again.

By the time we are finished with each other, I am shaking, leaning into his embrace as if it's the only thing that will keep me alive. I love him. I love his hands, tattooed and veiny and perfect. I love his eyes, streaky and unclean and omnipotent. I love the way he looks at me; I drink it like wine. I love the way he touches me like I am an antique.

Ocelle Galler has brought me back from the dead.

I lie on my side facing him, my face close to his chest. We smell like sweat, we smell like each other. I don't mind.

We don't say anything. I just hide from the rest of the world with him, feeling as light and happy as a feather.

Sometime in the middle of the night, Ocelle gets up to go to the bathroom, leaving behind only a quick kiss on my temple as a notice. I hear him shut the door behind him, and the water starts to run. I yawn and head back to sleep.

When I wake again Ocelle is still gone.

"Ocelle," I murmur as I sit up. "Come back to bed. I miss you."

No response.

The old familiar feeling sets in. The dread. I hear Cal's voice from down the hall, scared as a rabid dog: *Stars.*

No. That night, he hadn't called me Stars.

He'd said *Aster.*

I stand and make my way to the bathroom, which still stands closed. I try the knob and, to my horror, find it unlocked.

"Ocelle," I say breathlessly, my hand still leaning against the doorframe. I don't push the door open because I don't know what I will see, and I dread finding out. "Ocelle, I said come back to bed. Don't act like you didn't hear me."

Nothing.

I urge myself to stay calm. *This isn't like Cal*, I tell myself. *This isn't like that.*

Summoning all the courage I can, I push the door open, and my world ends for the second time.

TWENTY-FIVE

I sit in the passenger's seat of Lily's car, her cardigan wrapped around my shoulders. My fingers, trembling, are still raw and bleeding from where I'd scratched at Ocelle desperately, trying to evoke pain in him, praying to God he'd sit up and complain that I was hurting him. All I'd succeeded in doing was splashing tub water everywhere. He'd been in about an inch of it, still wearing his socks and his sweats, his eyes closed. He'd reminded me of that one woman — the most beautiful suicide ever, they'd said — who looked like she was asleep more than anything.

And that damn slip of paper they found clenched in his fist, the one source of vitality in his whole body: that little scrap of a to-go receipt on which he had scribbled *SING GOOD*.

The driver's side door opens and Lily appears, holding one coffee in each hand. She slips one into my grasp. "It's decaf," she says.

I look at her. She rests her coffee between her legs and pulls a ponytail holder off her wrist, yanking her hair behind her impatiently.

I try my drink. It's exactly how I like it because Lily's my best friend.

Without saying anything she reaches over and takes my quivering hand. "It's okay," she says, not looking at me. "I love you. It's okay."

Outside, I see nothing but the early light of dawn rising over the hospital's roof. Annabel must be inside right now, talking to someone.

Lily taps me on the shoulder, and I turn to look at her. She brushes some hair behind my ear and fixes my cowlick. "You're all messy," she says, a tad playful. "It's been a rough night for you, hasn't it?"

I nod. I can't talk at the moment. I screamed so loud, so raucously, and fell to my knees, which ache even now. My throat still throbs. The coffee helps.

My hands tremble as I check my phone. I message people I never would have messaged about something like this. To Camilla I say *hey, something bad happened again.* To Violet I say *i forgive you. i love you and i forgive you.* And to my father I say *maybe i really will come home someday, dad.*

"This sucks, Stars. I know it does," Lily murmurs.

I nod again.

"You're going to be okay. I'm not going anywhere, and neither is Annabel."

I nod for the third time. I know she is telling the truth. She and I have an interesting, beyond-best-friends-by-now relationship: she's the person I call in a panic whenever I find the love of my life dying in my bathroom.

If I had a nickel for every time...

"Maybe I'm cursed," I mumble, my voice raspy and broken. "Maybe I'm just doomed."

"Don't say that."

I finish off the dregs of my coffee and leave the cup in the cupholder. I lace my hands together, waiting for them to calm. They don't. I picture Annabel inside, talking quietly with people in scrubs.

For a long time nothing happens. I sit in Lily's car, completely immobile. All I think about is him: if he's gone yet, when will he go, when will that precious life fade from mine — how my thumb had found his forehead, that soggy *SING GOOD*, how everything had been falling apart since the moment I met him.

I find myself wishing I had played the piano for him.

Don't get me wrong, you're a monster on the guitar, but...

I start to cry. Loud, sopping tears. I feel Lily's hand on my shoulder.

"Hey," she says softly. "Stars. It's alright." But it isn't.

"Aster," Lily tries again. "Please look at me."

I do — and when I do, I'm startled to find that her own eyes are lined with tears. She pushes my hair back and sucks air between her teeth.

"Please." Her voice is quiet, as gentle as a lotus. "I am begging you to stay with me here."

Shakily I nod. I start to dry up. I've always had problems crying when other people are crying — especially if that other person is Lily.

A couple hours go by. We sit in silence. After a while Annabel emerges from the hospital's front, looking tired and cold, tugging on the lapels of her jacket. She knocks on the door, and Lily rolls down the window.

My entire body seizes up when I see Annabel's face: with her jaw clenched, her mouth a thin line, there's no telling what the prognosis is. I have no idea what is to be hoped for, what is to be wished against. The last time I was here it didn't end up going so great.

Lily reaches through the window and grabs Annabel's hand. "Annie," she says sincerely, "please give us good news."

Annabel looks at her, blinks, looks at me — and says, "Ocelle's gonna be fine."

I immediately start to cry again, smothering the noise behind both of my hands. This is really when I start sobbing, uncontrollably, I mean, hitting my hands against Lily's dashboard, fighting down bile. Annabel and Lily do not try to stop me. They just watch.

And when I'm done, I say, "I want to see him."

"Later," Annabel promises. "Let's go get something to eat first, let's talk about a couple things."

I can't believe this. He's okay, he's fine, he's not dead, no one is going to have to bury him. I did not sit in the dark and hold his hand until the flatline cut through me. I did not hold him close to me and watch his throat, gorgeous and motionless, falter without a faint green pulse. I did not help him hobble around the apartment, I did not spoon-feed him oatmeal, I did not do any of the waiting or the wishing or the dreading that I had done so long ago. I was not doomed. I had not lost him.

I am alive, and the man I love is alive, and I am whole — and maybe the man I love is not so whole, but I will help him to be wholer than he was.

. . . .

After we get some food, Lily drives me back to the hospital. I'm finally allowed to see him. My stomach churns with what I might say, what he might say. He could be angry at me; then again, he'd kissed me goodbye only the night before. I have every right to be angry at him, but somehow anger fails me now in the name of relief. As I walk down the white hall, Lily a couple steps behind me and a nurse a couple in front, my hands begin to sweat.

Finally I make it. And there he is, alive, perfectly and utterly alive, looking out the window at a couple of nesting birds. A shaved head, the shadow of a buzz passing over it. Naloxone. And, as the door opens, a swiveling neck, beautiful and strange, and eyes that find me — and glow with delight like the city lights.

Lily and the nurse leave us alone.

At first I just stand and look at him, and he looks at me too. He looks absolutely nothing like the man I met at Conan's all those years ago, all the necklaces and mascara and rings. Here he looks like a human being, not a god cast down from the sky. Here all of Ocelle falls away until all that's left is the man I'm in love with, the man I would do anything for, the man who put me back together.

I take a step forward. "Hello, Ocelle."

He shakes his head and smiles at me, the same smile as before. He holds out a hand like we're meeting for the first time. "That's so pompous," he says. "You can call me Adam."

TWENTY-SIX

H e's the same person he was. Effortlessly charming, poised and graceful, as easy to understand as your ABCs. And at the same time, complicated to a fault, spastic and *everywhere*, a beautiful amalgamation of all the best and worst parts that can make up a person. He is so loudly himself; he always has been.

He lets me hold his hand. I sit by his bed and he tells me all about it, all about his thought process and how he had left me there, sleeping. It was the worst thing he's ever done, he says. He says I looked so peaceful lying there, my eyes closed, my bare back beneath the warm covers. It broke his heart, he says.

It had been that damn conversation with Kento. They'd called each other names and said horrible things that I'm surprised I didn't hear from my perch up in Adam's old bedroom. Still, the two had parted with the agreement that they would never speak again, and Adam felt so blindsided that the only way to fix it was to turn everything off, leave everything behind — me included.

I kiss him again, and then I kiss him some more. I don't understand how I ever could have been ashamed of loving someone this much. I think perhaps I always knew but after Cal went away I forgot. I was scared. I am not scared anymore. I love loudly now.

"You don't have to worry about Kento anymore. Never again."

"Get me out of here," Adam says softly into my shoulder. "Take me home with you."

"No. Not yet."

"Why not?"

"Get well," I advise him. "I want you to be well before you come home. There's a couple of loose ends to tie up."

"Like what?" he challenges, his eyes still lagging.

I run my thumb over his knuckles. "I'm going to move," I hear myself say. It's the first I'm hearing of it. "I'm going to get a new apartment,

closer to Annabel and Lily, and we're going to put the band back together once you're better, and everything is going to be fine."

Adam cups my face in his hands. He studies me with all the love in
the world. "Is that really what you want?" he asks softly.

I nod. "It's time for a new chapter, y'know."

"I agree," he says. "I'll wait for you."

I kiss him again.

. . . .

I've quit my job at Conan's and put my life in boxes, standing in an
empty apartment cluttered with the remnants. My keyboard has
come out from the closet, sitting expectantly on the barren carpet floor,
not hooked up to anything. I'm just here, in the shell of my home, in
socked feet on the same floor where I'd danced with not one but two
beautiful men, men who'd adored me and accepted me and, above all,
let me sit next to them and share fruit with them. Lily is helping me
move, griping that she regrets showing up in a short skirt. Annabel is in
the U-Haul. Violet is in the other room, sorting through my filing cabinet, picking what things are most important to keep.

In my lap are Adam's big orange blanket, his favorite shift, a couple
of vials of nail polish. Things he asked me to grab for him and take back
to him. He'll be in rehab for a long while, and while he's gone I'll be
setting up shop at our new home, an apartment in the artsy part of the
city — something Adam will just adore when he comes back. I can't
wait for the future. I can't wait to see what it holds for me, for Adam,
for Mothic Wreckage, for all of us.

"Hey," Lily says behind me. I'm sitting on the ground. "You ready
to go?"

I take one last look around. Lots of dinners were held here. Lots
of crying happened here. Cal lived and died here, but I am not saying
goodbye to him. I never will. He and Adam are the most important

parts of my life, and I'm not giving in to the idea that saying goodbye is necessary.

I stand, holding my stuff. "I'm ready."

I follow Lily out and I don't look back.

· · · ·

The new apartment is a lot smaller, as it's all I could afford, with warm walls and an extra bedroom. A guest room, perhaps, and a spare closet to store all of the keepsakes from our old life. I hang Cal's art and Adam's sticky note doodles on the walls. Therese mails me a Polaroid that she took of all four of us so long ago, back during the early days. Mothic Wreckage was so young then, just a brief scattering of ideas, the product of three drunken idiots on Rigby's couch. Now it is this.

I look at the photo. We're all standing by our tour van. Adam's arms are around me and Annabel, who, uncharacteristically, is smiling. I am, too, but I'm hugging my middle like I'm nervous. Kento is next to this clump, his muscular arms folded, a grin tugging at his face. It fills my mouth with a bitter taste to see his face again. But for better or for worse, for a long time he was Mothic Wreckage's drummer, and I had to hand it to him: he did a good job.

I take the Polaroid and put it on our new fridge. Adam will see it right when he walks through the front door in a few months, and I know he's just going to love it.

Of course not everything is perfect, peachy keen. I know that. But Adam lived — and I'm on such a high. It finally feels like stuff might start making sense. It feels like I might belong to something, to someone, to a whole group of people. It feels like I've made Cal happy.

· · · ·

The three of us sit on the couch, all in a row. I'm holding a box of Chinese takeout in my lap, and Annabel is speaking.

"So," she says. She looks around at us. "Mothic Wreckage."

"Mothic Wreckage," Adam echoes sagely. His hand fidgets in mine, but he is otherwise still.

"Do you..." Annabel shrugs. "Do you guys want to try again?"

Silence.

"Try again," I repeat, tasting the idea alongside my lo mein. "Would it really be that easy?"

"I think it would be risky, personally," Adam says loftily. "But why the hell not, y'know?"

And that's the end of that. We'll finish the album, find a new drummer, and set off.

After Annabel leaves, Adam kisses me on the balcony. Then he sweeps me up off my feet and carries me back to the bedroom, where we're still unpacking even after all this time, and we collapse on the bed, huffing with laughter.

I run my hand down the side of his face. I kiss him everywhere: his eyelids, his temples, the corners of his mouth. I am enamored.

"I have a surprise for you," I say.

His eyebrows shoot up. "Oh, yeah?" he challenges. "What would that be?"

I wriggle out of his grasp and stand, depositing myself at the keyboard. And I play the song that I've been working on: the song about Cal. The song about Adam. "Flower." I let it overtake me, I let the memories drip down and fall apart. Piper. Losing my family. All of it.

I play a song for the men I love.

When I finish, my eyes on the keys, I feel Adam's hands on my shoulders. He kisses the crown of my head and leans down to whisper in my ear.

"What?" I laugh, feeling his breath tickling my cheek.

"I knew you were a piano guy," he murmurs.

TWENTY-SEVEN

I finish packing down all my suitcases, trying to take up as little room as possible. Adam's trunk is massive, a huge waste of space. Annabel has only a little carpetbag. Lily's is so small that it's in her lap up front. Therese is a similar story.

"Would you please hurry?" Annabel calls back to me. "You know we have to be out of the state by tonight, right?"

"Just give me a second," I grumble, giving the luggage one more push. When it's clear it won't be moving anymore, I shut the van's back doors and slide in next to Adam and Goodwin, our new drummer.

"Alright, boys and girls," Stan says warmly from the driver's seat. "Round two. Here we go."

He drives us out of Colorado. I watch the grass roll by, turning less green and greyer as we near the state line.

It is time to live for the people I love. I thought that's what I had been doing, but I was living for myself, creating illusions like a crazed magician. I threw myself to the tops of the mountains to make sure they were all alright and lost my head in the process. I'd been living to impress them, to make them love me. Now that era is over, and now I exist in their honor, holding myself as a god the same way they did.

By the time we reach the Borealis in Utah — an old tour stop, reiterated — I am exhausted. Adam and I share a room. Lily and Annabel share a room. It feels so painfully memorable that I almost roll up my jeans to check my knee, to see if it's still as bruised and ruined as it had been the first time around. Instead, I am new. Untouched skin. And Mothic Wreckage is new.

The next night is our show, the first of the new tour. We play some new songs from the album. Looking over to my right and seeing him is all I could have ever hoped for, all I could have ever dreamed of. I couldn't have asked for anything better.

And during the encore — "Castle of Girls" — I look out at all of these people, these people who love me so much they can hardly stand it. Annabel. Lily, offstage, cheering. Goodwin, behind me, playing the drums like he'll die if he doesn't. Stan and Therese. Everyone in this crowd, the men in patterned, loud shirts and women with jewels at the corners of their eyes. My parents, as much as I hate to remember it. Cal. Adam. Aster.

I look over at the thin body, the shadowy scalp, and he sees me looking. He smiles.

I smile too.

Thank you to Rachel Hermes, Ani Corbett, Sami Gade, Jessie Lucas, Venus King, Belle Slate, Kieran Crane, and Lucy Nichols for the never ending support. I also extend my thanks to Adam Blackwell, Alex Martinez, Will Osgood, Lucy Sugawa, Carissa Clarcq, Emily Cook, Laura Pitner, and Abby Leman for being amazing beta readers. Thank you to Sonder Akina for helping me decide Ocelle's star sign, and thank you to Sam Sherven for forever being in my corner. Thank you to Austin Civatte for being an older brother, author's best friend, and the best visionary ever all in one. In that same vein, thank you to Layn Mayfield, a younger sibling whose daily writing encouragements cheered me endlessly. Thank you to Sophia Blackwell, what an amazing editor you are! Thank you to Jo McIntosh for being my wonderful teacher. A massive thanks to Hannah Hinze, my soul sister. I also want to thank Athena-Grace Petkas for giving me a creative outlet when I first started college. Thank you to Lilly Glancy, Mathilda Nicot-Cartsonis, Evangeline Herring, Anna Fulton, Crystal Saffel, Sanjana Kumari, and Laiko Cayanan. Lastly I can't come all this way without thanking Bella Rothenflue; you've made the cover of my dreams!

Stars, Ocelle, Lily, Annabel, Kento, Cal — I love very few knuckleheads more than you bunch.

And a thank you to my mother — who, for a while, was the only one out of the two of us who believed I could have ever gone this far. (And a thank you to my father, who never read this book but ought to have been able.)

About the Author

Anya Nagle is a nineteen-year-old author based out of Austin, Texas. When she isn't slaying the dragons, she is chasing after her very stupid cat Orphie or attending university classes as a writing major. You can find her on Instagram at @anyaanagle.

Milton Keynes UK
Ingram Content Group UK Ltd.
UKHW020630220124
436466UK00020B/1084